T5-CQC-025

"SO YOU THINK YOU'RE TOUGH?

I'll show you what tough really means!" Calico Charlie flashed a gun and struck Blondy with the butt. The blow split his scalp and knocked him to his knees.

When Blondy Terrance, known as the Streak, came to Jasper Valley, he was a happy-go-lucky cowboy. A month later he was the most feared gunman in the territory. But Blondy had never killed anyone! A series of coincidences had earned him a reputation for violence he never deserved.

Then Calico Charlie came to town—determined to prove he was the slickest handler of hot lead in Jasper Valley.

Books by Max Brand

Published by POCKET BOOKS

MAX BRAND

THE STREAK

PUBLISHED BY POCKET BOOKS NEW YORK

POCKET BOOKS, a division of Simon & Schuster, Inc.
1230 Avenue of the Americas, New York, N.Y. 10020

ISBN: 0-671-41576-X

First Pocket Books printing January, 1953

10 9 8 7

POCKET and colophon are registered trademarks
of Simon & Schuster, Inc.

Printed in the U.S.A.

Contents

CHAPTER 1

In Different Directions

"BACK to Arkansas" was the song on the phonograph. Blondy lay on his bunk motionless, waiting for the end of the words. His stomach began to pull in; his chest rose. He stared at the dusty sunshine which streamed through the cracks in the western side of the shanty. Then he turned his head and looked through the door over the familiar flat. He knew by name and ancestry every Spanish bayonet that stuck up out of that landscape. He knew every hitch and twist in the line of fence posts that walked across the horizon.

A creaking sound from the phonograph. The "repeat" mechanism was carrying the arm of the machine back to the beginning of the record. In another moment the voice would sing:

> *I cannot fail to hit the trail*
> *To maw and paw in Arkansas. . . .*

The hand of Blondy moved. His fingers touched chafed leather and then roughened metal. Something more than chance had put the holstered gun beside him.

He pulled it out and fired across his chest without aiming. A lot of little tin cans jingled together. The voice did *not* begin to sing.

Dust was flying up into the cracks of sunshine. Blondy sat up.

"It's funny," he said. "I never hit anything before. Nothing that size, I mean."

Bill Roan lifted his three long sections from his bunk, stood, strode to the end of the room, picked up the phonograph from the box it stood on, and shook it, gently.

A thousand little tin cans jingled almost musically. They kept on jingling for a moment after the machine was put down, and Bill Roan kept his head bent, listening when there was still no sound.

Buck McGuire, who had been putting on the records, ran his fingers through his hair. One ray of sunshine set a streak of it burning like red flame. After that, he picked up the other three records and started shuffling them aimlessly.

"I could pick 'em out in the dark, by the nicks in the edges," said Buck.

Into the silence came the endless barking of the prairie dogs.

"It sort of built up in me," said Blondy. "And then I didn't know what I was doing. I guess I'd been thinking for a long time about the fellow that sang that song."

"He just fired without aiming, and I saw him do it," said Bill Roan. "Like one of the old two-gun deadshot boys in Grandpa's time. Blondy, you ever hit anything before?"

"No," said Blondy.

"It's just one of those things, is all it is," said Buck McGuire.

"Speaking of prairie dogs," said Bill Roan.

"Who was speaking of prairie dogs?" asked Buck.

"Speaking of prairie dogs," said Bill Roan, aiming a glance at Buck down the long length of his nose, "they got their voices hitched to a spring in their tails so's they can't jiggle their tails without barking, and they can't bark without jiggling their tails. We got nothing to drown them out, now the machine's gone dead on us."

"I've got my guitar," said Blondy.

Bill Roan looked again at Buck and softly caressed the jutting red triangle of his Adam's apple.

"He says he's got a guitar," said Bill.

"Yeah. I heard him, too," said Buck. They both looked earnestly at Blondy.

"How old are you?" asked Bill Roan.

"Twenty-three, Bill."

"He says he's twenty-three," translated Bill Roan.

"Yeah. I heard him say so," said Buck.

"I'm sorry," said Blondy.

"We don't blame you. We blame God," answered Bill Roan. "How're we gunna put in the time between this and bed? How're we gunna get the sun down?"

"I've finished patching my overalls," said Buck. "I could

of lasted that job out for three evenings if I'd used the old bean."

"You could take the patch off again and stitch it smaller," suggested Blondy.

"He says you could take the patch off again and stitch it smaller," echoed Bill Roan.

"Yeah. I heard him say it," answered Buck.

He stood up, suddenly. He was a small man, but big with muscle when he moved.

"Do something, will you?" he asked.

"Yeah. Sure. What?" asked Blondy.

"Wait a minute!" roared Bill Roan. "Buck's got an idea."

"Yeah, I got an idea," answered Buck. "We can't be any more damn fools than staying out here to ride fence for Perry and Applethwaite. What I say is why not barge away from here. Yeah, and come back here a year from now. We'd have something new to talk about, anyway."

"It wouldn't make any difference," said Blondy. "Nothing ever happens to me. You have to read books to find the adventures."

"How many adventures could your stomach hold, kid?" asked Bill Roan. "You can't ride; you can't shoot; you can't even daub a rope on a cow; all you can do is stretch wire and straighten up loose posts. You birds are gunna stay right on here with me. It's Sunday; that is all is the matter with you."

"I'm going west to have a drink of that mountain-blue," said Blondy.

"I'm going south," said Buck, "all the way to New Orleans and ship on a tramp for the South Seas."

"What in hell are you gunna find in the South Seas except moldy bacon and no eggs?" asked Bill Roan.

"I'm gunna find some damosels, dummy," said Buck. "Where could you go, Bill?"

"Back to the ranch house," said Bill Roan, "and get hold of a couple of *real* men to ride fence with me."

"That's right," said Buck. "Then you'll be here when we turn up a year from now with something to talk about. You can tell us how good the fried beans have been. Hey, Blondy, you'll come back here the end of the year? What I mean, May eleventh sure and prompt?"

"Why should I come back here?" asked Blondy.

"Well, it's in the book," said Buck.

"I don't know," considered Blondy. "When I get away to the other side of things, I suppose it'll be just as well to come back to this side again. Sure, Buck. May eleventh."

"It's kind of something to do," said Buck. "Makes me feel like a kid again."

Sunset lifted the western mountains into great, black, ragged paws. Against the darkness Bill Roan could not see the jogging horse of Blondy, but still, to the south, he could make out the dust raised by Buck McGuire and his sorrel gelding.

Bill Roan kicked an empty tomato can into the distance. He made a cigarette and looked over his shoulder towards the darkening east. Then he went to the can and kicked it again.

CHAPTER 2

The Town of Jasper

MAY eleventh returned as hot as dry August, and through the shimmer of the reflecting heat waves Bill Roan watched a rider floating up from the south; first a mite, then a slowly traveling black stick, and at last Buck McGuire in clothes that were the twins of those he had worn away the year before.

"Hey, Buck, you little sawed-off bum," said Bill Roan.

"Hey, Bill!" said Buck. "What you think, boy? What you say about yourself?"

He dropped off his horse and gripped the hand of Bill Roan. "You doggone old long-legged stork, how many frogs you been catching, Bill? How was the fried beans?"

"Prime," said Bill Roan. "You gone and lost the skin off your nose, Buck."

"It started peeling and wouldn't stop. . . . Where's the kid?"

"He'll be showing up if he didn't fall asleep somewhere and forget the way back. How were the damosels, Buck?"

"Oh, all right, all right," said Buck. "The damn fools are always laughing—that is the only trouble with them."

"You really get to the South Seas?"

"I got south enough, brother; I got plenty south enough. I got as far south as coconut oil."

"How you mean?"

"They wear it instead of lavender water and talcum powder. They wear that damn oil so's you can see the stars reflecting on them."

"Go on and tell me, Buck."

"Wait till a long Sunday comes, will you? What burned down the shack?"

"You know that cross-eyed son-of-a-gun, Harry Dexter?"

"Old Pie Dexter's kid, ain't he?"

"Yeah. Harry come out here and rode fence with me. He had a jug of moonshine and took right to it the first evening. He said he wanted to wash the Spanish bayonets out of his eyes. And he went to sleep in his bunk smoking a cigarette. The first thing I knew was smoke. I got to Harry and pulled him out with the hair all burned off his chest. And the shack went to hell in a hurry. We got another dump three miles up the line in the hollow."

"Hotter there, ain't it?"

"Yeah, but easier to dig down to water; and Perry and Applethwaite would send a man to hell if they could save fifty bucks. Wait'll I leave a note for the kid, and we'll ride up that way."

A blackened stump of a jost still stuck out of the ground and, in a split of the wood, Bill Roan stuck a page out of his account book with an arrow pointing north and the words: "New shack in the hollow. Waiting for you, Blondy." Then they went up to the hut. A light Ford truck stood in front of it with a fat driver under the awning of the seat.

"Hey, Pudge," said Bill Roan, "what did you come out here to waste our time about?"

"I brought out a sack of potatoes and some self-rising flour and that king of junk," said Pudge. "Hello, Buck, I thought you was gone to sea last month."

"A year ago is what you mean," said Buck, "but your brain is as fat as your belly."

"There's a letter in there for a relative of yours, Bill," said the fat man, adroitly shifting the conversation. "Fellow called Esq. But it come to the ranch and the first two names are William Roan. So long, boys. Want me to tell the boss you're back on the pay roll, Buck?"

"You tell the boss . . ." Buck began, but the fat man drowned the rest of the answer with the roar of the engine and drove away. The other two dismounted, watching the kicking tail of the truck as it disappeared over the rough ground.

"Any fellow with a job where he can make a wind for himself . . ." said Buck.

They went into the shack. "They took and built it right after the model of the old one," commented Buck. "They even put in the same old cracks and the same knot-holes in the rafters. You wouldn't think they could remember a rat-trap as good as that."

"Here's the letter," said Bill. " 'William Roan, Esq.' and what in hell d'you think of that?"

"It's somebody sending you a bill for your uncle's funeral," said Buck. "They're always polite till they collect."

"Listen," said Bill, holding the open letter. "It's from the kid. Whatta you think?"

"Blondy was always cock-eyed," said Buck. "The education he got never had a chance to settle down in him and do him any good."

" 'Dear Bill,' " read Bill Roan, " 'I'm up here around Jasper, a bit hobbled and hardly able to get down there to the reunion. Anyway, the idea of meeting again was so that we could swap yarns, and nothing much has happened to me in the past year. Otherwise, I'd put it in the letter.

" 'Best wishes to you and Buck. I hope he got as far south as the damosels and didn't pick out one of sixty winters, even if she had a garland of gold on her head. Yours, Blondy. P.S. I'll be getting down there to the ranch, one of these days.' "

"It's a funny thing how the kid can remember books when he can't remember brands," said Buck.

"Or to close the corral gate."

"Or where he left his matches."

"Or how much change is coming to him. I never seen such a damn fool over the bar."

"You know it's only twenty miles across the Jasper Mountains down to Jasper."

"You ever been there?"

"I've seen it on the map. I've never been there and I never want to be. I seen Joe Maple after he been to Jasper and he said it was a place all full of sleeping cats, and when they woke up they clawed each other and went to sleep again. The last time the whole town woke up was back in the T-model days."

"We could jog over there and look up Blondy."

"The kid might of jogged down here, for that matter."

"He couldn't think that far away. Not unless the ranch was up in the clouds. Let's sashay up there and have a drink of Jasper beer and come back tomorrow morning. We gotta have a chance for a real talk, don't we?"

"Well, boy, come on and hit the trail. Leave me put the potatoes up on the shelf and I'm with you."

They jogged up the pass that wound through the Jasper Mountains, presently, a narrow range that jutted up like the dorsal fins of a school of sharks.

"The hell of the sea," said Buck, "is you can't wear a sombrero. I started out with one, all right, and the wind took and fed it to the fish the first day out. That's what done my nose in."

"Leave your nose in your pocket for a minute," said Bill Roan. "There's Jasper, I guess."

They had reached the high point of the pass and its shoulders swung back to give a closely framed view of the valley beneath. From the narrow flats by the river low hills rolled back, spotted brightly here and there with growing crops of grain or hay. In the widest stretch of level land a jumble of houses flashed the sunlight back from its windows.

"There's some trees, anyway," said Buck.

"Too ornery to pave a road," commented Bill Roan. "There's no kind of man-sized automobile that would go down into Jasper Valley. The automobile traffic splits and runs each side through the mountains. But somebody tells me they're going to get in a branch from the railroad. That'll rub off some of the rust, and you can see what kind of a tin-can Jasper is, anyway."

They followed only a winding trail, in fact, until they

were down on the floor of the valley. There the way widened, ungraded, the hoofs of the horses slipping through the deep dust into chuck-holes. Comfortable farmhouses sat back from the main road at the ends of tree-shaded lanes, every house surrounded by a dark island of foliage; and the whir or the dim clanking of a windmill was always somewhere inside the horizon of the senses.

"You know what it said in the book that day about the land of adventures?" said Bill Roan. "Well, this is the land of sleep. I could shut the old eye and fall right out of the saddle."

"I hear something that sounds like work going on," answered Buck. "Maybe not, but I think so."

Here the wind that blew down the valley fell away and they heard distinctly the chugging of an engine behind a grove of trees. With it came the faint chiming of steel blades, and of steel hammers falling, all softened by dis-·tance until the turn of the road brought them directly to the place.

It opened among the trees, long lines of excavations for foundations and yonder a section of wall rising. Men were working with pick and shovel, wheelbarrows, hammer on drill, trowels, horse-drawn scrapers, and a round-bellied cement mixer was turned by a donkey engine. An arch of white canvas over the side of the road proclaimed in great red letters:

DENVER AND GRANBY RAILROAD
JASPER STATION

Not far off a wooden sign read:

FOR BUILDING LOTS AND FULL INFORMATION AS WELL AS MAP OF THE PROJECTED NEW DIS-TRICT APPLY TO THE OFFICE OF PERRY T. BALD-WIN COMPANY, MAIN AND SECOND STREETS.

Yet another sign read:

WORK DONE BY PERRY T. BALDWIN COMPANY,
CONTRACTORS AND BUILDERS.

Bill Roan and Buck drew rein beside the road and watched the workers, each thinly veiled in a cloud of dust of his own making.

A boy with a haltered cow on a rope also had paused to lean on the fence and watch the station building. He had a foreign aspect because the visor was torn off his cap and the remaining beret had been stuck at random on the blond bristles of his hair. Sun had burned his face dark; wind had chafed it with lines of gray into an irregular pattern.

"What's the name of the cow, brother?" said Bill Roan.

"Jimmy," said the boy.

He turned pale, disinterested eyes upon them and then looked back at the noisy building scene.

"You mean *her* name is Jimmy?" asked Buck.

"She was named after me before she turned out like this," said Jimmy.

"A low-down trick," said Bill Roan.

"All cows is low-down," said Jimmy, without turning his head.

"He says all cows is low-down," said Bill Roan, translating.

"He says so, and he's right," commented Buck.

"I say so, and I *am* right," declared Jimmy.

"This Perry T. Baldwin is quite an hombre around these parts, ain't he?" asked Bill Roan.

"*He* says so," answered Jimmy.

"Kind of a big-hearted bird, anyway, giving away land to the railroad. I never heard of anything given to a railroad except a black eye, up to this," observed Buck.

Jimmy extended his arm, pointing to the spaciousness of a large idea. He said: "Yeah, he gave away this land that the railroad is building on. But look at two hundred more acres that he's got here. Worth fifty dollars an acre, a month ago. Now he splits it into twenty lots to the acre and sells those lots at a hundred dollars a throw. That's two thousand an acre, or nineteen hundred and fifty clean profit except for the gab he spends on the deal. Two hundred times two thousand is four hundred thousand bucks, minus ten thousand for the land, and that gives you three hundred and ninety thousand dollars for Perry T. Baldwin. *Who* gives him all that money? The suckers that didn't have the sense to make the railroad build right in the middle of Jasper."

"Jimmy," said Bill Roan, "you sure can figure it."

"I got a milk route and I sell wild blackberries," said Jimmy. "You gotta learn to figure when you do these things."

"Jimmy," said Buck, "you seen around Jasper a kid by name of Blondy about six feet high, twenty-three years old, with a pale pair of eyebrows, and weighing about a hundred and seventy pounds?"

Jimmy turned his head at last and stared.

Bill Roan assisted: "Got a kind of a cock-eyed, lost look around the eyes, and sometimes talks like a book. Never can carry his matches and cigarettes papers and Bull Durham all the way across the room in one trip."

"You mean," said Jimmy, "the fellow that tames wild horses and can shoot the claws right off a flying hawk? You mean the gunman?"

Bill Roan laughed.

"The kid I mean," he said, "can hardly stick to an old mule; and he couldn't hit a barn unless the barn was held right still by somebody. Come on, Buck. We'll mosey on into the town. Where you get good cold beer in Jasper, Jimmy?"

"You get good beer at Flynn's and cold beer at Pete Reilly's," said Jimmy.

CHAPTER 3

Wanted for Murder

WHERE the cows wore trails around the first house in Jasper, the lanes of the town grew up. At least, they looked like lanes or streets from certain angles, but again they were simply trails through the jumble of houses, sheds, windmills, and shanties that made up the town of Jasper, population fifteen hundred. Only Main Street was straight, and paved. It was two blocks long and ran from First Street to Third Street.

Here the stores, the two hotels, the moving picture house, and every other building of importance in the town were located. The County Court House was the exception. It had a block to itself and sat back behind a fairly ragged lawn with a dozen tall palms scattered about. The palms had been pruned too closely, and they sagged their heads all to one side. About their feet the grass failed to grow. But it was an imposing Court House.

"I know what it's like inside without being there," said Bill Roan.

"So do I," said Buck. "I can see the big brass spittoons standing around all handy in the hallways. You would not think that Jasper would have a right fine up-to-date Court House like that there, would you?"

Just before their horses trod the hard pavement of the Main Street, where half a dozen old automobiles were backed aslant between the lines of the parking place, they came upon Pete Reilly's saloon on one side of the street, and Flynn's exactly opposite.

"You want cold beer or good beer?" asked Bill Roan.

"Try the cold beer first," said Buck. "Besides Reilly's is in the shade, just now."

They watered the horses at the trough, which ran in three sections along the edge of Pete Reilly's big, permanent, roofed awning. Then they advanced through the swing-doors into the barroom. The smell of beer barrels and whiskey kegs soured the air. The floor had just been swept. The lines where the water had been scattered remained dimly visible. It was an obscure room with one unshuttered window giving a picture of cattle grazing on green pasture land, a windmill beside a trough with a wide black margin of mud where the water had overflowed, and in the background a straw stack with one side carved away and glittering with fire and gold in the sun.

All the rest of the room was dark, and the darkest thing in it was the face of Pete Reilly behind the bar with a pair of black handle-bar mustaches sweeping down as far as his second double chin. His eyes never winked. The eyebrows met above the nose and angled outwards and upwards.

"We hear you got the finest beer in town," said Buck. "Let's have a pair of the tallest."

Reilly, stooping silently behind the bar, placed upon it

a pair of glass mugs that might have held two quarts apiece.

"Hey!" said Buck. "Glasses, brother, not mugs—"

Reilly did not smile. But his mustaches drew back a little as he filled a pair of glasses, ruled the bubbles off the top, and passed them onto the bar. Bill Roan and Buck lifted the drinks to one another.

"In your eye, Bill."

"A long life and a wet one, Buck."

They drank.

"How about it?" asked Reilly, his black eyes dwelling on them.

"C-c-colder than ice cream!" said Buck.

"Some folks eat my beer with a spoon," said Reilly, with the same unmoved, intent face. "Flynn, the poor fool, ain't got an ice house. And he ain't got the brains to cut the ice to fill one."

Bill Roan, sipping his beer diligently, said: "You know a kind of wall-eyed kid about twenty-three years old around Jasper? Been here maybe short of a year. Kind of handsome looking with pale eyebrows and looks a long ways from home, mostly."

"You mean The Streak?" asked Pete Reilly.

"Streak of mud, maybe," laughed Buck.

"Friend of yours?" asked Pete Reilly, picking Buck's fifty cent piece off the bar.

"The kid? Oh, sure he's a friend," said Buck.

Pete Reilly shoved the fifty cent piece back across the bar. He pointed a finger like a gun at the door. It was with his left hand that he pointed. His right hand fumbled for and found something heavy beneath the bar.

"Get out!" said Pete Reilly.

"What?" asked Buck, sticking out his bulldog chin.

Bill Roan took him by the shoulder. "Come on, Buck," he said. "All this damn beer does is make your teeth ache, anyway."

He got Buck to the door before the short man turned and shouted: "You ain't a bartender. You're a damned undertaker."

"Get out!" said Pete Reilly, his finger still pointing like a gun.

They untethered their horses and moved them across to the hot sun that slanted under the awning of Flynn's place.

"I'm gunna go back," said Buck. "I'm gunna go back and slam the big bum just once on the chin."

"That guy is sour," said Bill Roan. "The only time to fight a sour guy is when it means something. And what does it mean to get into a fight about a bird called The Streak? That poor fat-head of a Blondy is what we want to find."

"Maybe, maybe," said Buck. "That fool of a kid never would bring nobody no luck. But it was being asked to have a fight and sort of backing down. That's what eats me."

"The thug had a gun under the bar," said Bill Roan.

"I got a gun, too," said Buck.

"Aw, listen, Buck. Be a fool if you want to, but don't go and be a damn fool."

Buck permitted himself to be led into Flynn's saloon. It was a brighter place than Reilly's. Along the walls hung colored advertisements. Fresh, damp sawdust cooled the floor. And in a corner three men were drinking beer around a small table.

"Now pipe down about the kid," said Bill Roan. "He's gone and got himself in wrong some way. Just pipe down about him. Leave me do the talking."

"I don't want to talk about *him*. I don't care if I never lay eyes on him again. I want to talk about beer and Reilly's," said Buck.

There was a fat little bartender with a bald head as red as his face and a big blue vein running across the top of it.

"Are you Flynn?" asked Buck.

"That's me, partner," said the fat man.

"You keep frozen beer or something that a man can drink?"

Flynn beamed upon them.

He set about filling two glasses unordered.

"You been to Reilly's," he decided. "A couple of years ago he discovered ice and went kind of crazy. He sells you a stomach-ache with every glass."

"And when you drink your beer over there," said Buck, "you find the damned black face of Reilly in the bottom of the glass."

The beer came out of the spigot in a creaming, hissing stream.

"Is it steam beer, brother?" asked Bill Roan.

"It's the best kind of regular beer," said Flynn, "and it's chilled by nature, partner. Chilled with fresh spring-water that rises in my own backyard, yonder."

He filled the glasses. A collar of white an inch deep stood up on top, bulging above the rim of the glass. They drank.

"Chilled?" said Bill Roan, lowering his glass. "He says it's chilled, Buck."

"Not too much to kill the fine bitter flavor of the hops," pointed out Flynn.

"Not too much to kill the taste of the hops," translated Bill Roan.

"Anyway, there's no Reilly in it," said Buck.

"I been hearing things about a tall young fellow up this way," murmured Bill Roan. "Pale eyebrows, good natured sort of a lost look. Don't seem to know what he's about, half the time. Kind of handsome, in a way."

"Friend of yours?" asked Flynn, growing very sober.

"I wouldn't say that," said Bill Roan. "Just kind of wanted to meet up with him."

A chair pushed back in the corner of the room.

Flynn, bending, lifted from beneath the bar a big poster ornamented at the top by full-face and profile pictures of "Blondy" Jim Terrance.

"It's Blondy!" breathed Buck.

Bill Roan said nothing. He was reading aloud in a dull, stunned voice the caption which ran beneath the picture.

WANTED!   WANTED!   WANTED!
WANTED!

FOR THE MURDER OF
PHILIP B. COLES

"THE STREAK," OTHER NAMES UNKNOWN.
HEIGHT SIX FEET, EYES BLUE, WEIGHT ONE
HUNDRED SEVENTY, HAIR BLOND, MANNER
PLEASANT, AGE TWENTY-THREE
$2,500 REWARD.

The figures had been crossed out and in their place had been written: "$5,000."

"Five thousand dollars!" said Bill Roan.

A footfall had been crossing the room. A powerful young fellow almost as tall as Bill Roan loomed at the bar and rested a hand on the edge of it. His eyes burned into the face of Bill Roan.

"How would you like the spending of that much hard cash?" he asked.

"Why, brother," said Bill Roan, "anybody could use five thousand without a lot of pain, I guess."

"Don't 'brother' me, you dirty damned headhunter!" said the big young man.

Bill Roan licked his lips.

"That's fighting talk," he said quietly.

"If you were twice as many pounds as you weigh, I'd use my hands on you," said the stranger. "But if you've got tools for any other sort of fighting . . ."

"Hold on, Harry!" said the bartender. "Maybe they're *friends* of The Streak."

The other two men from the corner of the room were striding over the floor, calling out: "Don't start anything, Harry. You two back out of here before Harry starts breaking you up."

They came crowding in on Harry.

"If you back down, I'll take on the big porker," said Buck.

"I'm not backing down," said Bill Roan. "I've got the tools, and I'll use them if I have to. But I want to tell you that we've bunked and fed with Blondy for a whole year at a time."

"His name ain't Blondy. It's Jim," said Flynn. "The Streak's name is Jim. You boys got it all confused. There's not going to be any trouble about this."

"His name is Blondy Jim Terrance," said Bill Roan.

"Wait a minute," sang out Harry. "Wait a minute, everybody. Let go of me, you two. Stranger, would you put up your hand and swear you are not hunting for the blood money?"

"I'll do better than that," said Bill Roan. "I'll shake yours if you're his friend. This is Buck McGuire, another old chum of Blondy's. We got the wrong idea in Reilly's place. He asked us out of his saloon when we said that we were friends of Blondy."

"Did he do that?" cried Harry. "I'm going to tear the damned black whiskers off his face right now!"

His two companions clutched him. He brushed them away with a huge double-armed gesture and ran towards the door.

"Harry! Harry Layden!" shouted fat little Mr. Flynn. "What did you promise The Streak?"

Harry Layden already had knocked open the swing-doors, but the last words stopped him. He stood for a moment with one hand resting on top of half the door, the other half banging back against his thick shoulder.

At last he turned, breathing hard, a bright new devil still shining in his eyes.

"That's right, Harry," said one of his friends. "The Streak signed you up for the quiet life. You can't let him down can you?"

"I can't let him down," agreed Harry Layden.

He went back to the bar and dropped his elbows on it, put his face in his hands.

"I've got to keep on taking it and smile!" he groaned. "I've got to lie down like a yellow dog and let every rat in Jasper run over me on the trail of The Streak. They're going to corner him and shoot him in the back. I know what's coming! They're going to murder Jim while I stand by with my hands tied . . . tied by *him!*"

Flynn reached across the bar and patted the big shoulders.

"Stand up and take it with a grin," said Flynn. "They haven't got Jim yet. They're not going to get him if his friends stand by him. The only question is, are we standing by? What more can we do? You tell us, Harry, and we'll do it."

"I think you will, Flynn," said Layden. "You *are* a good fellow."

"We're having a drink on the house. Whiskey, boys. Beer isn't good enough for this round," said Flynn. "Stand up and take it, Harry. Take your places, boys."

He spun out the glasses. They ran winking down the bar from his expert hand, wheeling exactly into place before each man, and coming to a halt in a little tottering dance.

Before they were still Flynn was sloshing each glass half full of pungent whiskey.

"I'm going to give a toast with this one," said Flynn. "You boys wanta hear a toast?"

"Make it a short one," said Harry Layden. "I want the whiskey more than I want to listen to talk."

"You *got* to listen," said Flynn. "Boys, I'm asking you all to drink to a man with a hard fist and a soft hand. You're gunna drink this, or go dry, to a man that never was beat by wild horses or men, a man that's got a straight gun and a straighter eye, a man that may have a dark past, but he's got a clean heart, a big heart, a heart that never said 'no' to a friend, a man that never seen luck he couldn't smile at, a man that'll die the way he lived."

By this time Harry Layden was standing stiffly erect with his glass raised in a sort of permanent salute.

Flynn, like a clever political orator, seized on the emotional moment to lower his voice at the climax, instead of raising it.

"Gentlemen," he said, "I give you the man whose friendship is an honor to me. The Streak!"

They drank. And Harry Layden smashed his glass upon the floor.

CHAPTER 4

The Streak

BIG Harry Layden took Buck and Bill Roan by the elbows and stiffened their arms with the strength of the grip.

"It may be the whiskey working," he said, "but I believe what you've told me. You're friends of The Streak. And I wish you'd tell me how long you'll be around town."

"Why, we just wanted to see Blondy . . . and then we thought . . ." began Bill Roan.

"Listen, partner," said Harry Layden. "You mind not calling him 'Blondy'? It sort of bothers me. It sounds a little soft."

"He says it sounds a little soft," translated Bill Roan.

"He says right," said Buck. He swallowed. "For a fellow like The Streak, it sounds soft."

"If you want to see Jim," said Layden, "I don't promise anything. It's not too easy. But it might be done."

"We'll step along to the hotel," said Buck, "and then you might let us know when . . ."

"You'll step where?" asked Harry Layden, smiling. He laughed upon them both from his magnificence and height. "You'll step to a hotel, will you? What would Jim think of me if he heard that two of his old friends slept in the hotel? You're coming home with me, and no more arguing about it."

There was no more argument. The three of them rode out of Jasper through the late afternoon slowly, in the old Ford of Harry Layden. Tall Bill Roan held the lead-rope of his gelding, to which Buck McGuire's mare was hitched. The two horses crowded out to one side to avoid the dust that puffed and boiled out from the wheels of the automobile.

"This Philip B. Coles, that they hang on the neck of Jim," said Buck McGuire. "How might that have happened?"

"How might that have happened?" exclaimed Harry Layden. He exploded in such a rage that he forgot the driving of the car and let it snake in wide meanderings from one side of the road to the other. "Hell and fire, didn't a hundred men in Jasper Valley owe old Coles money and hate him because they owed it? What have they got against The Streak except that the bullet that hit Coles smashed in right between the eyes? I know that not many outside of The Streak can shoot as straight as that; and I know that he *was* seen going into the Coles place that evening. But why jump on him when there were twenty others that would almost have died themselves to see Philip B. Coles dead? What have they got against The Streak except that he's a dead shot?"

Bill Roan turned an eye of agony towards Buck.

"He's a dead shot," said Bill Roan.

"Yeah—dead shot," said Buck McGuire, choking.

"There's the Coles place now," said Harry Layden.

He pushed on the brakes with a sudden energy that staggered the little car crookedly to a halt.

Bill Roan could see a sweep of hillside that had once been garden but had turned with time and neglect into straggling patches of shrubbery. The white face of the house glimmered behind a cloud of slender poplars.

"I remember when Mrs. Coles died, and the old man started to let the place go to hell. He planted those poplars that year and wished that they'd grow so tall and so thick that he'd never have to see a human face again. Well, that's where the fools say The Streak committed murder. You see that corner window in the tower, that one with all the scroll-work carved around it? That's where old Coles used to sit. Everybody in town knew his light up there on the hill.

"If you wanted to talk to the old codger, you stood on the ground under the window and hollered up to him. Sometimes he wouldn't answer. You could hear him moving around, but he wouldn't come to the window. Other times he'd lean out the window and talk to you. Now and then he'd invite somebody to come in."

The thick clouds of white dust which the car had knocked into the air as it skidded to a halt now overtook it and drifted a fog across the eyes of Bill Roan and Buck. Layden started the machine again. In his angry impatience he made it jump like a horse under the spur.

"The fools say that because The Streak was asked into the house on the evening during which he must have done the job . . . There's hardly anything else against him. Nothing much except the neat way the bullet was put exactly between the eyes."

"What do you mean by nothing much?" asked Buck McGuire.

"Well, The Streak went out of town that night, after the killing of Coles. He just went out for a ride, the way anyone might do. And he didn't come back until the next morning. You'd say, a sort of funny thing to do, wouldn't you? But you fellows, if you know anything, know that The Streak isn't like other men. He's different. That's all. Besides, people were making a big fuss over him, and he was tired of the fuss. People had been keeping up that fuss for too long a time, and The Streak was tired of it all. So he slipped away and dodged the big dinner that night at the Perry Baldwin house. The unlucky part was that that *happened* to be the night that Coles was killed. You can see how it was."

"Sure," said Bill Roan. "And folks had to think that Blondy . . . I mean that Jim, or The Streak, or whatever you call him, had killed Coles. And that he had gone out into the country to bury the loot, and then that he'd come back to town with the money safely put away. Did anybody follow his backtrail?"

"Yeah. It was followed," said young Layden grimly. "And out where the sign of The Streak led, they found some money cached away. But you can see how that would have happened. After suspicion fell on The Streak, the real murderer went out there and planted the stuff."

Layden sighed profoundly. "You know how it is," said Layden. "A fellow like The Streak . . . too big for most folk to understand him. He's too high above the rest of us. What can you do about a man like that? Why, just give him your faith. Be a little blind. That's all that you can do."

Here Layden jumped the car from the roadway into the entrance of a long, narrow drive, lined with poplars so old that they had turned ragged and some of them were dead towards the top.

"How did it happen?" said Buck McGuire, glancing behind Layden towards the long, blank face of Bill Roan. "How did it happen, just then, that people were making so much fuss about The Streak?"

"Why, you know," said Layden. "After a thing like the hold-up of the Allentown stage, people naturally get a little excited. I mean when one man comes charging out of the woods and tackles seven two-handed fighters and gives them the run, it keeps people in this part of the world excited for a while. Maybe you fellows just take things like that in your stride."

Bill Roan said nothing. He had parted his lips for speech, but sound would not come; Buck McGuire, looking across in pained bewilderment, wore a similar suspended expression. And here the car slid out from the avenue of trees and came up in front of a ranchhouse typical of the Jasper Valley. The pioneers who first filled the Jasper Valley carried with them more ambitious architectural plans than most of the settlers in the region of the great ranches.

But in Jasper Valley there was plenty of timber and plenty of water-power for the cutting of it. So there was a fine splurge of building that lasted for a whole generation. All the houses were big, square-shouldered buildings, usually with a tower in the center, sometimes with a tower at each of the front corners, and a quantity of wooden carved work dripping from the eaves all around. The barn was sure to be almost as imposing as the house itself.

The Layden place was the type with only two wooden towers; but it looked like a castle out of a book, to Bill Roan and Buck McGuire. Some of the winter paint had boiled off in the sun or chipped off in the winter frosts, and the wooden columns of the veranda looked a bit mouse-eaten in places, but these little defects only made the place seem more homelike. On the veranda was a fine old gentleman with a flow of white hair, sitting in a rocking-chair. If he had had a white beard to go with his hair he could have been used to illustrate a Southern dignitary of 1860.

"That's father," said big Harry Layden, as they got out of the car. "Maybe you've heard of Foster Layden in your part of the world? Come on in."

They went up the steps, and Foster Layden gave them each a good, strong handgrip.

"Wait a minute, father," said Harry. "I want you to meet them all over again. I've only told you their names. I haven't told you that they're old friends of The Streak."

"My dear boys," said Foster Layden, "are you friends of The Streak? Sit down here! Harry, I think we have the makings of a mint julep somewhere in the house . . ."

"Where's Mary?" asked the son of the house. "She ought to know who's come."

"You can see her over there," said Foster Layden. "She's feeding Rocket—that's The Streak's horse, Mr. Roan."

Off there by the pasture fence in a flutter and flash of a white dress, they saw Mary Layden holding a bucket of grain between the top bars of a fence to a big red-coated chestnut horse that snatched mouthfuls and side-leaped away with his head in the air as though he expected to be struck for his thefts.

"He sure looks like a rocket," said Bill Roan. "He sure looks like he might explode."

"We pride ourselves on our horsemanship in Jasper Valley," said Foster Layden. "We have lagged behind the times, Mr. Roan. We have remained caught in back-water, I'm afraid. Modern days and ways roar and thunder in the distance, so to speak, and in Jasper Valley we remain, on the whole, contented with horse transportation; our roads, frankly, are too bad for motor vehicles. But the best of our riders couldn't sit on the back of Rocket. He began to grow more and more dangerous. At last I could not keep him any longer at this place. He was a continual red flag, a challenge to our high-spirited young riders. I think there were three broken legs, to say nothing of collarbones cracked and a thousand bruises, before I sent him into the back-country, to a little patch of pasture land I have at a shack up there. Then The Streak came along and heard about him—that was the end. Of course a forbidden horse was the only horse for The Streak."

Foster Layden laughed, softly and proudly.

"He just laid into that horse and busted him wide open?" demanded Bill Roan.

"As a matter of fact, he spent three days all alone up there in the back country. We didn't know what he was doing. And he turned up riding Rocket as casually as you please. Not as a conqueror, mind you, but as a friend. A very beautiful thing, I find it, when a dumb beast finds in the world a single understanding human mind."

"Yeah. Sure. It's fine," said Buck McGuire.

The big voice of Harry Layden had called from inside the house: "Mary! Oh, Mary! Hurry up! Friends of The Streak"

A girl should not show too much concern about young men, even the most friendly of them, but Mary Layden turned from the fence and came running and walking and running again, so that she arrived on the veranda out of breath and flushed and bright as a flower.

She gave Buck McGuire a warm welcome, but looking up the long, gaunt, bean-pole height of Bill Roan, she seemed to find it more possible to believe that he was indeed a friend of The Streak. She gave Bill Roan both her hands. She bent back her head and opened her eyes for him. And she said, still holding both his hands:

"I can feel that Jim is dear to you. Will you tell me

about him? Will you tell me everything about him? Some
time when you have hours and hours to talk? Has mother
met you? I'll bring her out. Oh, what a marvelous day it's
going to be!"

CHAPTER 5

Posse Cordon

THERE was to be no nonsense about merely staying for
dinner. They were to spend the night, and Mrs. Layden
went up the stairs with them to pick out the most comfortable room. She lodged them at last, in a huge chamber
from which three windows looked out, two on the mountains, and one on the winding flashes of the Jasper River.

At that window little Mrs. Layden stood for a moment
and then said with a sigh: "Jim loves this view. He'll be
happy to think of you in here. This is his favorite room,
you know."

She was a very brown-faced woman and she smiled only
with her eyes, as she smiled on them now before she left
the room.

"It ain't the kid," said Buck McGuire, when the door
had closed behind her. "It ain't any part of the kid. It's a
hell-raising somebody-or-other that sort of looks the same
way. You couldn't fit Blondy's skin over a bird like The
Streak. He's like one of those fairy tales. There's a bean-
stalk growing up here out of Jasper Valley as high as the
sky; and The Streak's somewhere up there among the
beans."

"No, it's Blondy," said Bill Roan. "There ain't any
doubt of that. Every way we describe him, it was always
the same; they recognized him right away."

"Then what happened to him?" asked Buck.

"Maybe there's something about this air of Jasper Valley," said Bill Roan. "Maybe in a few days you and me
will be picking our teeth with ten-penny nails and chewing
saddle leather for a light lunch."

"Maybe Blondy's taken and growed up all at once," said

Buck McGuire. "A couple of sunshines from that girl Mary would make anybody grow up."

"Grow up enough to take and murder an old man and plant the loot out of town and have it found where he put it? After a thing like that was found, how does he happen to have *any* friends left in this part of the world?"

"He struck 'em blind," said Buck. "Now leave us see how he'll strike *us!* Harry's gone to try to get hold of him."

The sun was pouring red gold on Jasper Valley when they finished washing and had sleeked their hair down with water. They came down the stairs stepping softly to keep the jingle out of their spurs and found Mary with her father and mother on the front veranda again. The mint julep, built tall and white, had been gathering frost. Bill Roan and Buck McGuire had one for an appetizer. And then they went back through the twilight, into the dining room.

There was fried chicken, hominy, a great green salad, freshly baked little biscuits crowned with gold and brittle as buttered foam, deep cups of coffee with individual pots of cream flanking, and there was an immense strawberry shortcake to wind up with, and more coffee to help it down.

"I forgot that eating could be so much fun," said Bill Roan. "You know how it is when you do your own cooking at the end of a day? You boil enough beans on Monday to last till Friday; and twice a day you take and warm up a chunk of 'em in the griddle with bacon fat."

"I don't think it ever was intended," said Mrs. Layden, "that men should live alone."

"A man is only a part," said Foster Layden. "Woman makes him a whole."

"I'm glad you said that," remarked Mary. "I think that's beautiful."

"On the other hand," said Foster Layden, "I don't know what part a woman could play in the life of a fellow like The Streak; like sitting on the hurricane deck with the hurricane blowing."

"*I* think," said Mary Layden, "that one day all the storm will blow away and leave Jim as still as twilight. Don't you think so, Mr. Roan?"

"Why, I always thought that," said Bill Roan.

A servant-girl, tall, long-striding, with the heavy jaw of
a pugilist, came into the room and said in her harsh voice:

"There's Mr. Perry Baldwin and twenty men at the door,
ma'am. They got guns."

Mrs. Layden gripped the edge of the table and closed her
eyes. Mary jumped up and ran to her. The three men stood
up.

"All keep your places," said Foster Layden. "There'll be
no trouble. Not between Perry Baldwin and me. Just sit
down again, boys."

Bill Roan answered: "I guess we'll go along with you,
Mr. Layden."

"Well, if you wish——" said Layden.

They walked behind him down the hall. Through the
screen doors of the veranda they could see Perry T. Baldwin complete in English riding togs with a crop in one
gloved hand and a cigar in the other. Behind him, on the
steps and on the ground in front of the house, stood a
crowd of silent men.

Layden pulled the screen open. The hinges squeaked as
the hinges of screen doors always do.

"Evening, Perry," said Layden. "Will you come in and
bring your friends along?"

"If you don't mind, Foster," said Baldwin, "a few of us
will come in. We'd like to talk over a certain matter with
you and your family."

"Come right in," answered Layden. "I'll call Mary and
her mother."

He went off down the hall after he had opened the door
to the sitting room.

Baldwin turned and said: "Thompson—Jed Walker—
Killigrew—Thomason—come in here with me, will you?"

Bill Roan edged an elbow into the back of Buck.

"It means business and bad business," he said. "This
here Baldwin is one of them empire builders."

"He's got a lot of new in those boots," said Buck, who
was rarely impressed. "Listen to 'em squawk when he steps
around."

The servant girl was lighting two oil lamps in the big
room as Baldwin trooped in with his cohorts. The Layden
family came last. Foster Layden introduced Roan and
McGuire to Perry Baldwin, who said: "We hear that you

two are friends of the man called The Streak. Is that correct?"

"That's correct," said Buck McGuire.

"It's not a reputation that will do you much good in certain parts of Jasper Valley," said Baldwin. "And it opens the subject which brought us here this evening. Killigrew, watch the door. Thomason, take charge of those windows and see that the blinds are not raised!"

Some of the people had been settling into chairs, but the crisp command that Baldwin put into his words straightened everyone again.

Baldwin went down to the end of the room and stood in front of the empty, black mouth of the fireplace. The image of his big, iron-gray head and solid shoulders swayed behind him in the mirror that went on up to the ceiling. He had on a stiff white wing-collar. The flesh under his chin pulled a bit at the cleft of the collar when he turned his head. He seemed too heavily dressed for that warm evening, but he seemed perfectly cool.

"I don't notice Harry with the family," said Baldwin. "Can you tell me where he is, Foster?"

"I don't know that I approve of this," said Foster Layden. "This, in a sense, is taking possession of the house of another man, Perry. I want to extend you every courtesy—but I can't help pointing out . . ."

"I don't blame you," said Baldwin. "This is a high-handed procedure. I want you to believe that if I take the lead in this, it's not from my own volition, but because I've been under a heavy pressure of public opinion to put an end to the scandal of The Streak."

"Scandal?" asked the small, high voice of Mary Layden.

Her mother said: "Hush, Mary."

Baldwin went on: "The very living scandal, Mary, of a fugitive from justice, a man who committed a terrible crime, a disastrous and brutal crime, my dear girl. A man who is being sheltered from the law by a number of misguided friends. Because he is young, dashing, and handsome, such fellows always have friends—for a while. I wonder if you will answer me, Foster, if I ask you directly where Harry is at this moment?"

"At this moment I cannot tell," said Foster Layden.

"Suppose I guess that after the arrival of these two

friends of The Streak, Harry has gone to find the criminal and bring him to this house?"

"You may guess what you please," said Layden very shortly.

"Our purpose," said Perry T. Baldwin, "is to remain here in this room, while the rest of my men form a cordon around the house. We commit the illegal act of forbidding any of you to leave this room so as to give possible signals by lights or in whatever other manner. In the meantime, I feel reasonably secure that when Harry and The Streak approach the house they will be apprehended."

Foster Layden walked across the room to Baldwin and faced him with deliberation. His face was almost as white as his sweep of long hair.

"I hear what you say, Perry, but I don't believe it. You don't mean that when Harry comes to the house, from wherever he may be at the present time, he will be stopped by armed men?"

"It's exactly what I mean," said Baldwin.

"You realize that anything could happen? The light's treacherous and very little of it now. Do you realize what could happen to my son at the hands of a mob?"

"It's not a mob but—" began Baldwin.

"Every group of twenty men is a mob," said Layden.

Buck McGuire had been staring at the frightened eyes of Mary for a long moment. Now he turned suddenly and walked up behind Layden. He intended to keep his voice low and discreet, but emotion strengthened it unduly.

Everyone in the room heard him say: "We don't have to sit down and take this. You've got Bill Roan and me right with you whatever you do."

Layden turned about slowly, as though it were hard for him to remove his eyes from the stern face of Baldwin. Then he put a hand on the arm of Buck.

"We'll have nothing like that," he said.

"All right," said Buck, staring at Baldwin in his turn. "We'll sit down and take it if you say to—but it's hard."

"For people who are—friends of The Streak," said Baldwin, "of course it's hard. I know this amounts to an outrage, Foster. I'll try to make amends for it afterwards. In the meantime I've given the most particular instructions that no man is to lift a hand in the way of physical violence in apprehending whoever approaches this house in the dark. The numbers of the posse will make resistance impossible, in any case. The thing will all be managed very smoothly, Foster. Try to have that much faith in me."

Little Mrs. Layden stood up and said:

"Perry Baldwin, I think that this affair will cost the lives of two men. And one of them is my only son. I think that it's due to the cruelty of your whole life, Perry, that you're here tonight. It's going to mean murder; I think you want it to mean that. I think you've trailed a cloud of poison through all the years of your existence."

Perry Baldwin put out both hands in a sudden, fumbling gesture. His face twisted with pain.

He said: "Harriet—my dear Harriet, what are you saying to me?"

"I've said what I feel," said Mrs. Layden.

She sat down and instantly removed her eyes and her attention from the room. Presently the usual faint suggestion of a smile was once more lingering around her eyes.

CHAPTER 6

One More Man

IT SEEMED that nothing could be of the slightest significance, nothing that men could accomplish, after that calm-voiced outbreak from little Harriet Layden.

Perry T. Baldwin threw up his two hands and let them fall back heavily to his sides. He said to his man at the door: "It has to be this way. Whatever we do for the public good seems to be done out of personal malice."

Outside the house someone screamed a sharp, quick warning. Hoof beats beat a tattoo followed by rapid explosions of a gun. Other voices began to shout; through them came a sudden uproar of hoofs thundering into the

distance. Men yelled all around the house, their voices
traveling away from it.

Then Baldwin, throwing up a window, let the noises
from the outer night flow more clearly into the room.

"Donohue! Donohue!" he shouted.

A screeching voice answered: "He shot his way through
—he's stampeded all the horses!"

Perry T. Baldwin ran out of the house with his other
men behind him. Their feet banged on the veranda as
though upon the hollow of a bridge. The earth muffled the
noise. Voices still yelled in the distance, dimly, here and
there. But the disturbance was dying out. The peace of
the night closed in like soft, dark water. The house of the
Laydens was still again.

No one had left the sitting room during the crisis. There
seemed no use, with the tide of disturbance sweeping
away from them.

Then Mrs. Layden said: "Foster, I think perhaps you
had better search the ground and see . . ."

Mary Layden cried out, suddenly stabbed with fear.
She crumpled up in her chair and began to weep.

Foster Layden was silently joined by Buck and Bill
Roan, but now, before they could leave the room with
the heart-broken sobbing of the girl behind them, a slow,
light foot-fall came up the front steps of the house. The
front screen creaked as usual, and then a voice called
cheerfully from the hall: "Hello, everyone. All the trouble
gone, or is there something still left in the house?"

Blondy himself stood on the threshold of the sitting
room and waved a hat of welcome to the people inside it.
He called out suddenly when he saw Buck and Bill Roan.

"This is great!" cried Blondy. "Bill, you look taller
than ever. Buck, here are the Three B's together again!"
He went on past them, exclaiming: "Why, Mary, what
have you been crying about?"

"I'm not crying now," she said. "The cowards! The
cowards! The cowards! I knew that a *hundred* of them
couldn't take you. I knew that you'd scatter them, Jim!"

"Jim, can you tell me where Harry is?" asked Mrs.
Layden. All the three Laydens were pressing close to
Blondy. He put his arm around the mother of the family.

"He don't look any different," confided the whisper of Buck to Bill Roan.

Blondy was saying: "Harry's all right, mother. He made me come right on to the house while he stopped over at the Shannon place to see if they had any fresh venison. Harry's always thinking about the things I like, you know."

"He shouldn't have let you come alone," said Mary angrily.

"Hush, Mary," said Mrs. Layden. "How could poor Harry know? I thank the kind God that both of you are safe! Dear Jim, did you hurt anyone? Are you sure that you're not injured?"

"Why, I'll tell you what happened," said Blondy.

"Now, Jim, tell the *exact* truth," said Mary. "Don't understate everything as you always do."

"It was this way," said Blondy. "I was riding up towards the house when someone sang out and asked who was there; then I saw figures growing out of the ground, so to speak, and the starlight glinted on gun barrels. I thought that I'd better get away pretty fast, so I turned my horse and got as far as that patch of brush near the windmill. But there they started shooting. I thought that a horse and man would be easier to hit with a bullet than a man on the ground, so I slipped out of the saddle into the brush; the horse galloped on.

"I saw him hit a line of horses fifty yards farther on. Those horses must have been tethered bridle to bridle or tie-rope to tie-rope, rather. The whole crowd of them went off at a stampede. The men went after them, shooting and yelling. You must have heard it all in here. That's the whole story."

Mary had picked the sombrero of Blondy off the chair on which he dropped it.

"Isn't *this* part of the story, Jim?" she asked, and holding forward his hat she pointed to a double hole which had been clipped through the crown.

Blondy touched his hair and smoothed it thoughtfully.

"That will let in air; a good thing for hot weather, Mary," he said, and laughed.

Mary Layden held out her hand.

"Jim, I want to see your gun," she said. "Show it to me this minute, like a good boy."

She reached for the holstered Colt on his thigh; but Blondy stepped back. "You don't want talking out of school, Mary, do you?" asked Blondy.

CHAPTER 7

The Streak's Reputation

BLONDY was given the room next to that of Bill Roan and Buck. He sat for a long time with them. Harry Layden came up with a bucket filled with ice and beer bottles but he refused to stay. "You old timers have a lot to talk over" he said. "I might make the wrong angles. Good night!"

"Now, kid," said Bill Roan, "let me see that gun of yours."

Blondy, with a chuckle, pulled out the gun and tossed it onto a bed.

"Don't chuck a loaded gun around like that!" warned Buck. "You act like the same doggone chump as ever. Don't you know a loaded gun is liable to—"

"That's the point," said Blondy, still laughing.

Bill Roan, breaking the gun open, gave it a shake. Nothing issued from the chambers.

"It ain't loaded with a thing but dust," he declared. "It ain't been used tonight. What you mean carrying a gun around without stuff inside it, kid?"

"What's the use of carrying bullets when you can't hit anything with them?" demanded Blondy.

Bill Roan opened a bottle of beer.

"He says what's the use of carrying bullets, Buck?" said Bill Roan.

"I heard him," said Buck grimly. "Now go on back to the beginning. How'd you get introduced to Jasper Valley as a sort of self-loading lightning-flash?"

"It's all been luck," said Blondy. "The craziest luck

you ever heard of. You go back to the day they held up the Allentown stage, for instance."

"Go on back and start there, then," said Bill Roan.

"I was coming over the hills, just riding in from Perry and Applethwaite's— How far away the old ranch seems."

"It begins to seem pretty far away to me, too," agreed Buck. "As if those Jasper Mountains kind of fenced one away from all the other sorts. Go on, kid."

"Well," said Blondy, "as I was riding down a thin sort of a trail through the woods, guns started crackling and bullets began to hum through the trees, going crick-crack through the branches, and thudding into the trunks. I gave a yell and pulled out my gun. I don't know why, because all I wanted to do was to make tracks—and I fired that gun into the air. The only bullet I've fired in Jasper Valley, no matter what they may say."

"Well, I'll be damned," said Bill Roan, filling a glass with beer and crinkling foam. "After that shot, what did you do?"

"Made that mustang hump, and I came out bang onto a highway where there was a big motor coach stopped and people lined up on the road, and down the road some riders making tracks as fast as they could leg, and piling up a big cloud of dust— You know what the Jasper Valley roads are like."

"We know," said Buck.

"The people there by the coach sang out to me not to chase the robbers because there were seven of them; and you can lay your money that I didn't do any chasing.

"And all at once I found that I was a hero, a single-handed damned hero, boys, that had delivered a flank attack on seven bad-men and made them run for their lives. The men all shook my hand. The women almost cried over me. And so I simply told them exactly what had happened and that I didn't deserve any credit. I mean, the idea of me posing as a man-killer was quite a laugh.

"But when I got through telling what had happened, everybody looked at me and shook their heads. And the minister who was along said that a modest man was the noblest work of God. And they made up a purse to give me, but I seemed to have been established on such a high plane that I couldn't very well take presents, you know."

"So you didn't take the purse?" asked Bill Roan.

"No," said Blondy.

"Always dumb," sighed Buck McGuire. "Go on, kid. That was the way you got introduced to the town as a hero, was it?"

"It was that way," said Blondy. "And the first thing you know, I was rather liking it. And then along came Foster Layden himself and told me that he had talked with his son, Harry Layden, and he was afraid that Harry had had a share in the holdup of the Allentown stage, and he wanted to persuade the boy to go to the sheriff and make a clean breast of it.

"He kept on buying drinks and I kept on listening and drinking the drinks and feeling pretty happy and then into the saloon steps a fellow as big as a house. 'There's Harry now,' says Mr. Layden. 'Harry, I want you to come here and talk to The Streak.' "

"How'd they come to call you The Streak?" asked Buck.

"The way my mustang streaked out of those trees with my spurs stuck into it," said Blondy. "That was the reason, I think. Streaking away on the heels of the rotten wrongdoers, and all that, you know.

"Anyway, there I was asked to take Harry Layden with the look of a grizzly bear about him, and trot him over to the sheriff! Why, I simply broke out in laughter, what with the queerness of the idea and the whiskey I'd been having. I slapped Harry on the back and said, 'You and I won't have any trouble, will we?'

"Before I could go on to tell him how far I was from making trouble, I saw that he was a little gray around the gills, and he said through his teeth, 'I know you're a better man than I am, but I'll be salted down with lead before I'll be kicked around even by you.'

"I said that I didn't intend to try anything—and that was the truth. But I felt a bit bigger, when I saw how he was acting, and I told him he really ought to come with me that moment over to the sheriff. And, boys, he turned a little whiter still, and if the sheriff wanted him the sheriff could come and get him.

"So I went across to the sheriff and explained that Harry Layden, like a fool of a kid, had ridden out with those thugs, not to help in the stage hold-up but just to be in on the excitement. Harry was waiting to be arrested in the saloon of Pete Reilly.

"The sheriff is Wallace Nash, and pretty much of a decent man. He shook hands with me and told me that an influence like mine would make Jasper Valley into a different place. As for Harry, I was to go back and tell him not to be a damned fool again, but to try to grow up. He the sheriff, would forget all about the Allentown stage.

"So I went back and found the two Laydens sitting like two stones. When I told them what Wallace Nash had said, they got up and sort of grabbed me, both of them. They started to walk out, when the bartender said that I owed him some money for beer while I was sitting in there before Layden showed up.

"That was true, but Harry Layden said that I couldn't spend any money in Jasper because my debts were his, and he threw the money on the bar. That led to some hard words; and pretty soon Pete Reilly grabbed a gun from under the bar. Harry caught that gun away as though he were picking it out of the hand of a baby. I thought that he'd make Reilly eat that gun before I managed to stop the fight; but Reilly had turned from a black rat into a dripping red one before Harry was through with him."

"That's the best news that I've heard in a long time," said Buck. "Go on with your yarn, kid. You certainly played in luck."

"I certainly did," said Blondy. "After that I seemed to be on the top of the world, so far as Jasper was concerned. I couldn't spend any money . . ."

"But how did you make any?" asked Bill Roan.

"Queer ways, when you come to think of it. For instance, Riley Partridge ased me to come out to his ranch, one day. He had about twenty Mexicans working for him, and the brutes were growing rambunctious. They wanted an increase in back pay, and better food, and they wouldn't leave till I arrived on the place, and Partridge lined up those black-faced natives and talked to them like a Dutch uncle. He kept pointing to me and telling them that The Streak would run the lot of them ragged if they didn't pack up and get off the ranch. I thought it was all a joke and began to laugh; but the Mexicans certainly packed and left in a hurry."

"They got you built up pretty high, kid, in Jasper Valley." said Buck. "I hope you never fall. What did this Riley Partridge pay?"

"I told him it wasn't worth a penny," said Blondy, "and that I couldn't have done anything, anyway. But he said that it was worth five hundred dollars to him to see any man laugh in the face of twenty black Mexican cutthroats with their knives ready and sharp. He made me take the five hundred, too."

"What was the next step?" asked Buck.

"I think the next thing that happened was when I tamed my horse, Rocket." Blondy shook his head. "That was a strange one," he admitted. "You see, I'd spent a good deal of time with Mary Layden, and she talked a lot about the wild horse that really was *her* horse, but it was too savage to be handled and was kept back in the country at the small farm, so that the boys wouldn't risk their necks trying to tame it.

"So I slipped out of there one time and thought that I'd gentle Rocket with patience. But there was no gentling of him When he even saw me sitting on the fence of his little pasture, he went prancing around and gave his watering trough a bang with his heels that opened a crack in it, and all the water ran out.

"I fooled around the place all that day and the next, trying to get that damned horse acquainted with me. But the third day I saw him standing in a corner with his head down and his legs braced apart, looking sick. Then it came over me that he was sick. Like a fool, I'd forgotten about the watering trough, and he hadn't had a drop of water for the three days!

"I went into the corral and he stood and looked at me with a dead eye. He only made one small attempt to savage me when I cinched up the saddle on him. I climbed onto his back and he walked with a stagger up to the watering trough. I kept on his back and reached over and worked the handle of the pump that spilled the water into the bottom of the trough. And he drank, and drank.

"After that, he was a changed horse. He simply followed me around. I let the water run out of the trough through the crack, and when he wanted another drink I'd go and pump just a little into the bottom of the trough and let him have it. He began to have soft eyes, like a dog. He's never so much as backed an ear at me from that day to this. So I nailed up the trough and pumped it full and rode back to the Layden place. They were a good deal surprised. I explained how I'd done the thing, but they only laughed at me. You see, when I tell the truth about the way things happen, the people in Jasper have made up their minds that I'm always just making small-talk out of a big thing."

"That's why they laughed tonight," nodded Bill Roan. "They thought that you'd sailed into that crowd single-handed and scattered them."

Blondy sighed and shook his head.

"I suppose they do think that," he declared. "I wish you and Buck would tell them that I'm the most ordinary sort of a fellow. It'll save me from trouble."

"We'd get ourselves murdered trying to explain you, brother," answered Bill Roan. "Like to oblige, but you know how it is. Harry Layden wanted to choke me only today because your name was brought up. What about the killing of old Coles, and who was he, anyway?"

"He was a rich man. All I know is that one day I got a message that he wanted to see me. I went and called on him. He said that he was in fear of his life. There was going to be an attempt on it, and he would pay me big money to come to his house and be a bodyguard.

"I told him that I'd think it over. I *did* think, and the more I thought, the more I realized that I was going to get my scalp taken off one day before long, the way things were piling up. I simply packed my blankets and headed out of town without saying good-by to anyone; because it would be too hard to say good-by to so many friends.

"But when I remembered Mary early the next morning, it was too much for me, and I came back. Afterwards, the real crook planted some of the loot on my back trail. That's all the truth as I know it."

Buck filled a glass of beer and poured it down his throat in one fine gesture. Afterwards he pulled out a brilliant bandanna and swabbed down the mahogany red of his face. He said:

"Kid, is there nobody in Jasper Valley that sees through you?"

"There's Mary," said Blondy.

"How you mean there's Mary?" demanded Bill Roan. "She gets a tremble in the lip and a tear in the eye every time your name is mentioned."

"She thinks that there's something dark in my past. Either that, or else I'm just lucky here in Jasper. Which is the truth. Every time I see her, I ask her to marry me. But she holds back. She seems to like me pretty well. But she wants me to come clean. And there's nothing much to come clean about. She thinks that some day terrible things will be known about me and then what sort of a heritage would she have for our children, besides being widowed when she's still young?"

Bill Roan said, "You wrote us down at the ranch that nothing had happened to you. What you mean by that?"

"I mean that I've done nothing. You can see that for yourself. Even when it came to the horse—why, he broke his own trough in order to make himself gentle for me."

CHAPTER 8

The Sheriff's Permit

LATE that night Buck and Bill Roan still were talking.

"Suppose that we leave him?" asked Bill Roan. "His luck will play out and he'll go smash."

"When he goes smash," said Buck, "it's gunna be in such a big way that all of his friends will go down with the sinking ship. I like Blondy fine, but not enough to go to hell for him."

"No," said Bill Roan, "but there's the girl to think about."

"Sure," agreed Buck. "There's the girl. But what could we do for her?"

"Find out who killed Philip B. Coles."

"Bill," said Buck, "the fact is that Blondy *did* kill Coles."

"Hey! Hold on! How do you make that?"

"I make it easy. When he talked about how he got money, he looked a little queer. Bill, I think he's been living on Coles' money all this while."

"You think that Blondy could do a murder?"

"Sort of by chance, maybe. But he killed Coles all right. And when he saw Coles dead, he couldn't help taking part of the money that was around."

"He never done it," answered Bill Roan. "I'll swear to that. And I'm gunna find out *who* killed Coles. That will clean up the kid's record and leave him inside the law."

"And who'll go back to the ranch? Who'll report to Perry and Applethwaite?"

"*You* can go back and do that, if you want."

"You're making a fool of yourself," said Buck. "Why?"

"For a few years back, there was always Three B's," said Bill Roan. "I'd hate to have it get down to only two of them left."

"True," answered Buck. "I never thought of that."

That was why Buck McGuire did not start back across the mountains towards the ranch, the next day. He accompanied Bill Roan, instead, when Bill jogged his horse through the dusty streets and tied up at the hitching rack, and besides, three half-wrecked automobiles stood in the shallow semicircle of the parking place.

"You could close your eyes and know it was a courthouse," said Buck McGuire, when they entered the big hallway of the building. "You could tell by the stink of the stale cigar smoke in the air."

A man went by in an alpaca coat with a pack of papers in one hand and an eye-shade pulled over his forehead.

Bill Roan signaled him for a halt. "You tell us where the sheriff is?" he asked.

The man in the alpaca coat laid a finger on his lips. "I'll tell you where the sheriff is," he said. "But don't you let on about it. Sheriff Wallace Nash is always on the right side of the fence." He went hurrying off, snorting with mirth.

"It's a funny thing," said Buck, "what a fool a man looks like when he laughs."

They found the sheriff's office around the first corner and to the left. A triangular sign jutted out from above the doorway and proclaimed the important place. Black letters on the white of the clouded glass invited them to walk in. They found an anteroom with a pair of benches in it, instead of chairs. On the benches sat a queer assortment—a Chinaman with a queue pulled over his shoulder, an adolescent boy with the clothes of a man, and a man-sized gun on the hip, obviously looking for trouble, a scrawny girl, yellow with fear.

"What can I do for you, friends?" said the deputy behind the desk. Then he started up, suddenly. "Wait a minute! You're the two that hit town yesterday—friends of The Streak? You come right in along with me. The chief will see you, all right."

He took them into a big office, with a big mahogany desk in the middle of it, and two big spittoons flanking the desk. And yet people had missed the orifices of those spittoons. They had missed badly. The bull's eye had been surrounded by yellow rings.

Sheriff Wallace Nash was a user of the weed. He sat behind his desk scraping the tops of his fingernails with a penknife. The sheriff had a pale, flat eye and a nose pushed to one side by the kick of a mule. His face was deeply lined. Into the furrows that ran down from the corners of the mouth a bit of the tobacco juice had run down. It did not dry. It was freshly moistened by an extra drop from time to time. Neither did the flood spread. It was a fixed watermark on the cheeks of the sheriff. He was a big man on the back of a horse, a small man sitting down. He was fiftyish.

"You boys know The Streak, do you?" he asked. "Well, I know him, too. I wish I knew him better. My job is to put him behind the bars. But I've got no heart in that job. The people know I've got no heart in it. If deputies want to swear themselves in as a posse and go chasing The Streak, I have to swear them in, that's all. Everybody has a right to his own opinion. When a man won't stand trial, other folks have got a right to use their guns on him, pretty free. Anything I can do for you fellows?"

"Thanks," said Buck. "Who killed Philip B. Coles?"

The sheriff showed no surprise. He began opening drawers of his desk and looking into them. Then he drummed on the blotter and looked at the wall. Finally he lifted the blotter and pulled out a slip of paper.

"One of these," he said, showing it.

"You got fifty names down there," said Bill Roan.

"I took 'em out of the card catalogue of Coles after he was killed," answered the sheriff. "That card catalogue mentioned all the people that owed money to Coles and how much they owed and when they had to pay it."

"You make anything out of the list?" asked Bill Roan.

"I been making," said the sheriff. "There's twenty of them that ain't got any alibi for where they was on the night that Coles was killed."

"Nobody has alibis in a country like this," said Buck, "unless horses and cows could be swore in as witnesses."

"You can't go and arrest twenty men for a murder that only one of them did," said the sheriff.

"Sure you can't," sympathized Buck.

"You boys want to clear up things for The Streak, I guess?"

"That's what we aim to do."

"You go as far as you like."

"Where you suggest that we start?"

"The scene of the crime is where the detectives always start in books. You better go look around the Coles place. Though I've known a whole lot of crooks to get clean away while people were standing around, looking at the dead man."

"Suppose that we went up to the Coles place, would we get in?"

"I'll hand you a note to the caretaker. Maybe *he's* the real killer, for all that I know. He used to be the servant of Coles, in the old days. The only servant in that big house, and he hated his boss bad enough to want to kill him. No doubt about that."

"Sheriff," said Bill Roan, "if you got any clue that you can pass out—we're old bunkies of The Streak."

"Boys," said the sheriff, "if I had a clue, I'd follow it

myself. The man that can clear up The Streak is going to be the most popular fellow in the valley."

He dipped a pen into the big inkwell and cocked his head on one side while he started writing. He drew the capital letters out carefully, and scribbled the small ones. When he had finished, he squinted his eyes and looked at the paper like an artist at a picture, Afterwards, he nodded approval of him work and signed with a flourish. He blotted his signature, folded the paper, put it into an envelope. Then he stood up and presented them with the document.

"Boys," he said, "I want to tell you something. You're likely to have some hard times if you stay around here. Most of the people like you fine because you're friends of The Streak. But twenty per cent of the people are going to hate your hearts. Those twenty per cent have most of the land and the hard cash in Jasper Valley. Layden is an exception. So is Riley Partridge. Now, I hope you clear up The Streak. Sure I hope you do. But I hope that some of the crooks around here don't railroad *you* into jail before you've been long on the way. So long. Good luck."

They left the office, and as the door closed behind them they could hear the sheriff saying, "Tom, bring in that cross-eyed little fool of a kid that thinks he's gunna be a desperado."

In the open air Bill Roan said, "The sheriff's all right."

"You better put that in the paper," said Buck. "Because he'd thank you for saying it."

"The trouble with politicians," said Bill Roan, "is they get so soaked in tobacco smoke and so boiled up in tobacco juice that they got no more brains left than smoked hams, after a while. I been rubbing the palm of my hand against my hip for five minutes, trying to get the political grease off of it."

They jogged their horses back through Jasper to the grounds of the Coles place. They passed through the broken gateway and up the wind of the driveway until they were in front of the house. A scrawny lawn fronted the house, and the lawn was fenced in with what had once been a hedge of firs. But the firs had turned into young trees, and the trees had been gnawing at one another for years. The strongest ones were elbowing the weaker to death. There were time-eaten holes of brown through whose bars one could look freely.

The veranda steps creaked under their feet. The boards of the veranda groaned under their weight. Then Bill Roan was dropping the knocker on the metal plate. The knocker was the bronze head of a lion from which one ear had been chipped away.

They could hear no footfall approaching the door, but presently it sagged open and jerked to a stop when it was only a few inches ajar. A strong chain held it from opening wider.

Through the gap they could see a narrow, wizened, pale face set off by the bristles of a black mustache.

"Well?" said a high-pitched voice.

"We got a pass from the sheriff to see the house," said Bill Roan.

"Passes don't get you into this house," said the other.

"Are you Jeffrey Tenner?" demanded Buck.

"I'm him."

"Here's the letter from the sheriff."

A thin hand snatched the letter. The door slammed so heavily that a long-drawn echo could be heard walking deep in the house, and running lightly up the stairs.

CHAPTER 9

Jeffrey Tenner

"IT LOOKS like murder; it feels like murder; it sounds like murder," muttered Bill Roan. "What'll we do? Kick the damn door down?"

"We'll go back to the sheriff and get permission to use an ax."

But here the door opened, again only a crack.

"Are you McGuire?" asked thin-faced Tenner.

"Yes," said Buck.

"Swear?"

"Yes."

"Lift your hand and swear."

"I swear I'm Buck McGuire."

The door was suddenly loosed open. "If one of you is honest, the other is likely to be," said Jeffrey Tenner. "You want to see where Philip B. Coles died, don't you?"

"We want to look around and see that, mostly," said Buck.

"Come with me," said Jeffrey Tenner.

He led the way across a big hall. Double doors that opened into a dining room showed the chairs stacked on top of the table. The roller rug had been stripped away from the stairs that climbed up from the hall to the higher floors of the house. On the landing hung a painting of a bridal couple, the woman with whalebone fingers holding up her lace collar and stiffening her neck, the man with black mustaches that shone like grease.

"Is that a picture of Coles?" asked Bill Roan.

"No; that's a picture of young Phil Coles," said Tenner. "Philip B. Coles was mighty different from that."

Tenner stood on tiptoes to reach. He stretched so that wrinkles sprang into the back of his coat. He stood pigeon-toed, tapping with a long nailed forefinger here and there.

"Philip B. Coles had pouches here, and another one under his chin. There were black smudges under his eyes. His eyebrows grew out long and bushy. His mustaches were always lop-sided, because he chewed the left side while he was making up his accounts. You never would of known Philip B. Coles married. This was what she died of—and Philip B. Coles was all that was left."

"And what you mean by that?" asked Buck.

But Tenner was continuing up the stairs with quick, mincing steps that had a surprising lot of bounce in them and he did not seem to hear.

They went up two flights, turning each time through big hallways that had been dismantled completely, with furniture marks against the walls where the paper had been sheltered from the light and had not faded like the rest.

So they came up three last steps to a door at which Tenner rapped, and then listened.

He made a little grunting sound before he turned the knob of the door and pushed it cautiously open.

There was no one inside. There was only the round tower room, completely furnished, and obviously as it must have been before the death of Coles. It was more an office than a study. It had a filing cabinet with a long, narrow face; there was a little round-cheeked safe in the corner of the room; and the desk was open, showing pigeon-holes stuffed with papers. The only decoration in the room was a picture of the young Mrs. Coles, still in the lace collar, still with her neck stiffened by the whale-bone fingers.

"Sit down there, Mr. McGuire," said Tenner.

He pointed to a chair in front of the desk. McGuire took it. It was a swivel chair with a tricky spring in the back of it, apt to let one suddenly tilt. Buck tilted and saved himself by grabbing the edge of the desk.

"He was in here," said Tenner. "He was sitting there. It was along in the twilight. I'd come up and lighted the lamp for him. That lamp on the side of the desk. A gentleman like Philip B. Coles wouldn't have thought of lighting a lamp. His brain got so busy that he forgot about saving his eyes. When he took to his accounts, he didn't need much light, though. He could feel his way through his figures. That filing cabinet didn't matter very much.

"He remembered everything. Everything that he wrote down about money, he remembered. For twenty years, he could tell just what he'd given me every Christmas. Sometimes it was five dollars. Sometimes it was seven and a half. Never more than seven and a half."

"Not a very good kind of a bird, was he?" asked Bill Roan.

"He didn't think about being good. He thought about making money. And hell inside his house. Hell inside his house! Hell!" said Jeffrey Tenner through his teeth.

"Look here," said Buck. "This is a free country. You could have got another job if you didn't want to work for him."

"Who says I didn't want to work for him?" demanded Jeffrey Tenner. "Who else would I have worked for? I seen him kill his wife. Who else would I have worked for afterwards except to see the heart eaten out of him little by little? He had a rat inside him; and the rat kept eating him; and I could watch."

He put his head back and set the room ringing with a screech of laughter.

"How'd he kill his wife?" asked Bill Roan, biting his lip as he watched the servant of the house.

"He beat her with words. He was one to start yelling the house down. She used to watch him like a frightened dog. And he'd beat her with words and make her crawl to him. He made a damn dog of her. She'd come crawling. Then when he seen what he'd done, he'd be sorry. I've seen them both crying. Both of them! But the next thing it was all over again. She couldn't have any children."

Bill Roan wiped his face with his bandanna

"Speaking about the way Coles was killed," he said, "how do you think it happened, Tenner?"

"I don't think how it happened. I know how it happened," said Tenner. He pointed to the window.

"I'd been up here and lighted the lamp. And he was there at the desk. Somebody called from under the window. And Philip B. Coles stood up and went to the window. He looked out. It was deep twilight. I was back in the kitchen cooking bacon and new-boiled potatoes. And Philip B. Coles was up here looking out of his tower window. And he seen the heads of the trees looking at him, and the color in the sky beyond the trees. And the black night spread out over the ground. He seen all that, and the rat in his heart bit him sharp and deep. And he seen the man under the window and told him to come up."

"Some say that it was The Streak that he asked to come up," said Bill Roan.

"Who do I care came up?" snapped Jeffrey Tenner, showing his yellow teeth in a grimace. "Only I know that the man came. And they talked for a while—"

"How do you know that they talked for a while?" asked Buck.

"There!" said Tenner.

He pointed to a piece of paper whose corner was stuck into the leather binding of the blotter.

"When he was talking," said Tenner, "he was always making little figures. They didn't mean anything. You see? This looks like a little cottage with the smoke coming out of the chimney. And here's a horse and a saddle on it, and there's a mother hen with her wings spread out. He learned to make those little drawings when he was a boy in school, and whenever he was talking with anybody he had to have paper and pencil, so's he could keep his eyes down, because if he looked up the other man might see too much."

"So he did that while the man was talking to him?"

"Of course he did. That paper was on the middle of the desk when I found him dead here."

He pointed to a dark spot on the rug.

"That's where he fell out of his chair. That's where his head hit the rug. And the blood dripped from the hole in his forehead. He was mighty particular about keeping things in his house clean!"

Again the unexpected screech of laughter made Roan and Buck McGuire start.

"But he knew that he was going to die long before the bullet smashed through his brain," said Tenner.

"How did you tell that?" asked Buck.

"Look at the arm of the chair. The end of it. The end of the left arm of that chair where you're sitting. There where the carving is—the deer's head with the horns. You see there?"

"I see," said Buck. "What's that tell you?"

"See anything?"

"I see the deer's head, all right."

"Anything on it?"

"Sure, varnish."

"And nothing else?"

"A spot of dirt is all."

"It ain't dirt."

"What is it, then?"

"Blood!"

Buck got out of the chair with a shudder, and stood staring down at it. "Yeah?" he said. "Blood?"

"I saw it when it still was red and I didn't clean it away," said Tenner. "I left it. That's how I know that he was tasting his death for a while before he died. He saw the gun out. He saw the face of the man behind the gun. And he gripped the arms of his chair hard, and he talked hard. And he squeezed hard. He begged for his life. He begged God and the murderer to spare him. How I would have liked to be here to listen! I keep saying over to myself the words that he must of spoke! And he gripped the arm of that chair so hard that the skin of his hand broke, and the blood ran a little. And then—then he didn't feel it any more. The gun boomed. He felt the smash of the bullet. You think maybe that he could feel the bullet tearing through his brain? I dunno. I keep wondering about that. I guess he didn't feel anything except the bullet. And then he started toppling out of the chair, with his head over to one side, dead."

CHAPTER 10

Perry T. Baldwin

ON THE wall of Perry T. Baldwin's office hung the picture of "Greater Jasper." It was thoroughly well painted, under a blue sky with the familiar ridge of the Jasper Mountains looming in the near distance. One looked down from a slight angle, like a stooping bird, or an ascending angel, upon the regularly drawn streets of the city to be, with its big railroad station on the one hand and its noble municipal park on the other.

On the wall facing the great painting of the city of the future appeared a naked plan in which the lots of Greater Jasper were measured out in white on a vast sheet of blue paper. Here and there appeared rectangles marked off in red. These were the plots which already had been sold or contracted for future delivery. It was nowhere stated how many of those red enclosures represented the land which had been reserved by the Perry T. Baldwin Company, but there was more interesting news near by.

It was a table of prices of lots according to their distance from the railroad station. Two of those lists had been scratched out and only the third list was unaltered. This showed how the prices had risen all along the line during the past three weeks. It seemed to show, also, how outside capital was invading the valley in order to buy right and left on the new site.

Perry T. Baldwin, at his desk between the picture and the map, had two assistants to point out features at will when there were clients in the room, and nearly all day long there were such clients. They came from all parts of the valley.

There were ranchers, small farmers, storekeepers, and even some of the old prospectors stopped steering their burros through the upper mountains on the trail of the gold of tomorrow and descended into Jasper Valley to take a sniff of the air of a strange adventure, the making of a new city. The word had gone out. Eureka was just there around the corner.

At this moment there were half a dozen prospective clients in the room. Perry T. Baldwin had risen to meet them and had waved them to seats which ranged in a spacious semicircle before his desk. He was then somewhat in the position of a teacher.

Only stupid pupils would fail to learn the lesson of success from such a teacher.

Perry T. Baldwin's clothes and his clean, well-kept hands were those of one who does most of his business in an office. But his brown face and his high color were those of one who spends most of his time outdoors.

He looked like a man who could not be wrong.

The introductory talk already had been made, when a man said, "It looks like a fellow could have a mighty fine time in Greater Jasper, all right. But suppose that I was to move in off the farm and build a little house here for me and the wife, how would I get out to the farm every day for work?"

"That's a very usual question," said Perry T. Baldwin. "The point is that it's hard for all of us—it's hard for me—to realize how things will be when the new roads go in. How long is Jasper Valley, would you say, Mr. Stephens?"

"Nigh onto forty-eight miles," said Mr. Stephens, pleased to be asked.

"Nigher to fifty miles, from the crossing, to Portlee's old mill," said another voice.

"Call it fifty miles," said Perry T. Baldwin. "Now then,

how wide would you call it? An average of about four miles, say?"

"Call it four," several of them agreed.

"We live in a rather long and narrow world here," said Perry T. Baldwin. "But let me show you what is to take place. Right down the middle of the valley a road will run, straight as an arrow. That road, my friends, is going to be not more than two miles distant from the house of every man, woman and child in the valley. Do you see what that means? Horse vehicles will become a thing of the past. A man will step into his automobile, wind for a few moments along one of the pleasant lanes that lead from his house, and then turn out onto the surface of the broad highway, polished black by the whirling of a million tires. In twenty minutes he can pass from the farthest end of the valley to the town. He can be alighting in front of the great new station, or be shopping at one of the big modern stores on Main Street.

"Yes, my friends, it means more than that. It means that Jasper Valley, mounted on modern, cushioned wheels, will begin to pursue the standards of the rest of the world, will draw equal with them, and almost at a stroke will be out in the lead. Already men of capital from the outside are reaching out for part of our coming prosperity. But still I hold them back and postpone accepting their tempting offers, because I want Greater Jasper to be for the benefit of the men and the women and the children of Jasper!"

He struck the top of his desk a solid blow and then leaned back in his chair with a slightly embarrassed laugh.

"I want you to excuse me," he said. "The fact is that when I see the future of the valley I'm a little carried away. Thomason, point out the eastern and western entries of the highway, if you please."

Thomason raised the long, rubber tipped pointer and indicated a wide, parked avenue which entered the painted beauties of Greater Jasper from the east.

He said, "Starts right here, folks. Jasper Avenue runs in here and goes straight on through the city. It comes right up to the railroad station, here; and then it passes on in this direction through Main Street and the shoppin' district, and then it runs out here to the west the same's it comes in."

"Oliver," said Perry T. Baldwin, "will you indicate how the sales are going along Jasper Avenue?"

The man at the opposite side of the room raised his pointer in turn, and pointed out with it various red squares outlined along the course of the great boulevard.

"Those red parts are already sold, folks," said Oliver. "Seems like people can see right away quick what kind of a street it's gunna be that runs right on through the city from one end of Jasper Valley to the other. Seems like it's gunna be one of the most beautiful roads and streets in the world, and folks are hankering to get space alongside of it. More'n fifty per cent of the available sites already have been snapped up."

There were murmuring exclamations after this.

"I understand a man can get time from your company, Mr. Baldwin, if he wants to buy in the town?" asked one.

"Of course he can get time," said Baldwin. "The company has arranged the easiest terms in the world. I hope you'll all understand that the company is strong because it is working for the prosperity of Jasper Valley. And the prosperity of Jasper Valley is the prosperity of each and every man in it. The company looks upon every man in the valley as a friend, and as a partner to be helped and trusted."

This remark was so moving that one man began to clap his hands together and the rest instantly followed the example. There was a good, solid burst of applause. As it died away Perry T. Baldwin was still waving a hand that put away all personal sense of merit, and invited total confidence in the future.

A fellow said as the noise died down, "I got not a spot of hard cash, but I got four ton of hay in town ready for the warehouse. How would that be for a down payment?"

"I accept it," said Baldwin. "A man who begins in a small way is apt to be the one who goes on to the big things."

Another man said, "Now, speaking about the new highway—you mind tellin' me how everybody can get to it from each side of the valley when the Jasper River goes slam right through the middle of things?"

"True," said Perry T. Baldwin. "The Jasper River, as you say, runs through the middle of the valley. And of course neither its beauty nor its inconveniences have been overlooked. In fact, the river will be bridged at the vital points." He raised his voice and said, "At the vital parts, graceful bridges will throw their arches across the stream and carry the road swiftly on towards Greater Jasper."

"Don't those bridges cost a whale of a lot of money?" asked the doubter.

"They *do* cost money," said Perry T. Baldwin, smiling and nodding. "I'm glad you raised that point, because there is going to *be* money in Jasper Valley. Not only from the increased wealth of the developed land, not only because of the richness of the new city itself, but because of the harnessed waters of that very river of which you speak. When the upper cañon is dammed up, part of the electric power will be used to light the streets and the houses and the farms of the valley, but another part will be used to turn the machinery of powerful modern factories.

"For instance, why should the grain of Jasper Valley be shipped away at great expense? No, gentlemen, it will be turned into the purest white flour by mills located in our own city. Why should our cattle be sold at half the current value because of distant markets? No, gentlemen, the cattle will be butchered and the meat frozen and shipped from our own stockyards. Money? Yes, gentlemen, there will be plenty of money for the new Jasper, the Greater Jasper, and all of its needs!"

"I got to wait for the grain harvest," said another, "before I could make a down payment."

"My dear Mr. Wilkes," said Perry T. Baldwin, "don't you realize that to me your note will be as good as cash in hand?"

"That's mighty kind of you."

"I'd like to continue talking over the scheme with all of you," said Perry T. Baldwin, "but the fact is that I'm called away to an important meeting in my private office. Anything else you wish to ask about will be answered by Oliver or Thomason. They understand the whole business almost better than I do. I want you to ask them plenty of questions. I want you to make yourselves familiar with the entire idea."

He went out of the room followed by a buzz of appreciation and entered an adjoining office to be greeted by the buzz of a telephone. His secretary answered it, saying, "Just a minute, sheriff. I think Mr. Baldwin can be found in a moment."

He covered the mouthpiece with the flat of his hand. He was a pale young man with the look of a weasel about his sharp muzzle.

"Want to talk to him?" he asked.

"I suppose so," said Baldwin.

"How are things going?" asked the secretary.

"Slowly," said Baldwin. "I take loads of hay and promissory notes instead of good, hard cash. I'm putting pearls before swine."

"If you can fatten up those swine you might sell them out for a pretty good price, though," said the secretary.

Perry T. Baldwin let his eye dwell on the bold young man sternly for a moment. Then he decided it would be better to smile. So he smiled. The old saying goes that no man is a hero to his valet. The same thing goes for private secretaries.

Perry T. Baldwin sitting down to the telephone said, "Ah, sheriff. What's the news with you?"

"Not much," answered Sheriff Wallace Nash. "But I got some news for you. About The Streak."

"Have you got a clue to his whereabouts?" asked Baldwin, sitting straighter.

"No. But those two friends of his were in here. They got the look of a pair of pretty hard-handed boys, Baldwin. And they want to take care of the interests of The Streak. You know I gotta play friends with The Streak till the right time comes. So I gave them a pass to see the house of Coles."

"I'm glad you mentioned them," said Baldwin. "You give me an idea. Are they at the house now, you think? That's splendid. We'll make everything work for us. Glad you called up. If you play your cards close to your chest, you're the man who'll turn over The Streak to the power of the law."

"And have people call me a yaller traitor the rest of my life?"

"You and I have talked all that over before. I thought that it was settled."

"Well, I guess it's settled. Only I can't help thinking, now and then."

"Stick to the original idea. At least you won't lose any money by it. What are people saying, today, about that fracas last night? Are they laughing at the way The Streak walked through my hands?"

"They're not laughing. Part of the folks are swearing mad; and the other half are just nodding their heads because they don't think that either God or Perry T. Baldwin can handle The Streak. Good-by!"

Baldwin hung up the phone and sat for a brief moment in thought, though the secretary was saying, "The committee of the posse is waiting for you. Shall I let them in?"

"Go over to the Coles house," said Baldwin. "You'll find there or near there the two friends of The Streak who have just arrived. Know the look of them?"

"The whole town knows them."

"Do that for me. Have you got Calico ready?"

"He's in the next room, primed."

"Then let the committee come in."

CHAPTER 11

Calico Charlie

NOTHING gives to men a more mutual expression than anger. Five angry men walked in on Perry T. Baldwin. Their anger was not directed at him, but it made the promoter very distinctly aware of them.

He said, "What's the bandage around your head, Taylor? And you, Walters? Have you got that arm in a sling as a result of last night?"

Taylor said, touching his head, "Walters and I don't matter. But you know how Tucker is?"

"He's in bed, but he's going to get well," said Baldwin.

"The Streak only got three of us last night," said Taylor, "and not a single death among the three. I suppose we can call that luck. But I wanta know what dirty traitor gave us away to him."

Baldwin said, "I am not through looking into the thing. We know that there was a traitor? Do you really think that even a madman like The Streak would ride right into the middle of twenty armed men?"

"Sure," said Taylor. "That's his idea of a lark. That's his idea of the real fun of life."

"I think," said Perry T. Baldwin, "that I have found a way of qualifying his pleasure in life somewhat. Sit down, everyone. Make yourselves comfortable. I believe you all know that my entire future, my business prospects, everything I have in the world, is tied up in Jasper Valley. I have a great undertaking on foot in this place, and instead of good notices going out of the place, we are sending out word about The Streak! Word about murder, midnight escapes, and everything in short, that will warn honest capital away from the valley. Is that clear?"

A growl answered him.

"Finally it occurred to me," went on Baldwin, "that there is a way of fighting poison with poison. I have that poison in the next room. But before I dream of using it, I want to consult you. I think you're the most representative men in Jasper Valley, and I want to have your opinion: Do you think we are justified in hiring one of the most notorious gunmen to be found anywhere in the world, free, in prison, or waiting for the hangman's rope?"

There was a slight jingling of spurs as they stirred and looked at one another.

Taylor touched his wounded head, instinctively.

"Why not?" he demanded at last.

"Why not?" asked the others in a chorus.

"Very well," said Baldwin. "That's your considered opinion?"

"Sure it is," said Walters. But what makes you think that any *one* man in the world is gunna be able to handle The Streak?"

"I'll tell you why," said Baldwin "Let us give the devil his due. Let us admit that there is about The Streak a certain manly openness and carelessness.

"Murderer and villain that he is, there is a casual approach to life and its adventures for him. Am I right?"

"That's why half the people in Jasper Valley tie to him," said Walters.

"Well," said Baldwin, "the man I have in the next room is one with the cunning of a wild cat and just as much mercy. He has stolen on victims in the middle of the night, murdered, and gone on his way. That he is still at large is a terrible reproach to the law of our country. Another proof of the devilish and poisonous cunning of this man is that at the present time there is not a single charge hanging over his head. Shall I bring him into the room?"

"Bring him in," said Taylor. "I want to see him. We'll vote on him before his face."

Baldwin went to the door, knocked three times on it, and stepped back.

The door knob turned so slowly that the highlight which gilded it hardly trembled. The door pulled softly ajar, then came wavering open, as though blown by a draught.

Then, on the threshold, they saw a little man who vainly tried to add to his inches with extra high heels on his boots.

He was rather good looking and wore on his face a continual, ingratiating smile. It was only a second examination that showed how the prominent front teeth forced the lips back, so that the lines of the smile were involuntary as they were permanent. His eyes, too, which at first seemed pleasantly bright, began to appear pale and of a deadly fixedness.

He made a little step across the threshold and sidestepped. In this manner he put his back against the wall. He was dressed flashily, in a short Mexican jacket that was a good bit too loose around the shoulders and especially under the pits of the arms. It was towards those loosenesses under the pits of the arms that every man in the room looked with fascinated attention.

It was a voiceless whisper that said, "Calico Charlie!"

No one knew how he had the name. Perhaps it was from his shirt. It was of the finest silk but it was blue, with white dots scattered over it, like a calico print. No shirt of any other pattern would he ever wear. His luck, men said, he connected with those blue and white silk shirts.

He stood quietly by the door and turned his pale, bright eyes slowly, deliberately, from one face to another. He did not need two seconds to make every man of them look another way. After that his smile was not entirely involuntary. It began to be real, and some of the pink of the gums above the long white front teeth commenced to show in his smiling.

Baldwin said, "Gentlemen, this is Calico Charlie. He has come here to have you look at him. He wants to find out the terms. If you wish to employ him, what will you pay?"

"There's a five thousand reward on his head already," said Taylor. "Isn't that a high enough price?"

Calico Charlie cleared his throat and even touched his throat with a delicate hand.

He said, "No."

"Why isn't it enough, Charlie?" asked one of the five of the committee.

"Are you raising your price on me, Calico?" asked Baldwin. "The reward was to be yours—and we all were to help you in any way we could to come on the trail of The Streak. Wasn't that the agreement? Why are you asking for more money now?"

"Last night," said Calico Charlie.

"Last night?" said Baldwin.

Calico Charlie pointed to Walters. He turned and pointed his quick little flash of a hand afterwards at the bandaged head of Taylor.

"After last night the ante went up," said Baldwin. "Well, I think that there may be a ghost of a reason for that. Charlie, tell us how much more you want."

Charlie raised his left hand with the five fingers all extended.

"What?" demanded Baldwin. "Five thousand more? You want five thousand more for the job?"

Calico Charlie said nothing. He looked steadily at Baldwin. Only the eyes of Baldwin failed, in that room, to turn from his.

"Listen to me," said Baldwin. "The law will pay five thousand for him, dead or alive. We'll pay more to help out. But our main contribution is to cover this valley with people who will try to spot the Streak and keep bringing you word of him. In addition to that, when the time comes for the showdown, any man of us within reach will be your helper. Isn't that an advantage?"

Calico cleared his delicate throat again. "No," he said.

"Not an advantage?" asked Baldwin. He turned angrily to the others. "Well, my friends, what do you say?"

Taylor had his glance fixed hungrily on Calico Charlie. At last he burst out. "I say that he's worth the money. I'll put five hundred on him."

"I'll do the same," said Walters.

No one else spoke for a moment.

"Well," said Baldwin, "we'll raise what we can, and then I suppose that I'll have to make up the deficit. Calico, you've made some stiff terms. Are you sure you won't raise them again, later on?"

"No," said Calico.

At this, everyone in the room laughed, nervously.

"We'll have to let it go at that," said Baldwin. "It may be worth ten thousand to the valley to get rid of The Streak. Personally I think it will. But you're inclined to sell yourself at a luxury price, Calico, aren't you? You *are* a luxury, aren't you?"

"Yes," said Calico, and smiled again.

CHAPTER 12

Blood Money

BACK there in the house of Philip B. Coles, Buck McGuire and Bill Roan had continued, for a time, to stare at the carved arm of the chair, and at the dark spot on the rug.

"Any way of dying that's quick isn't so bad," suggested Buck.

"Aye, but think of him sitting there and waiting, with the gun at his head," said Tenner. He laughed again, without the screech in his voice but making only a whispering, panting catch of sound. His mouth opened wide. His eyes burned as he laughed. "Think of him knowing that he was gone! Think of him turning his eyes to the cabinet, there. Aye, that was when his heart caught fire like a piece of dead wood and burned to ashes.

"What's in the cabinet?" asked Buck.

"Look!" said Tenner.

He pulled open a drawer filled with cards five by eight inches.

Bill Roan took one of them and read—it was first in the cabinet—from the name at the top left-hand corner to the last signature at the bottom. There were several entries, under date lines, such as:

I promise to pay Philip B. Coles for value received one year from date with six per cent interest, eight hundred dollars ($800)

> (Signed)
> *Aaron Wolf Aaron.*

Two diagonal red lines ran through this promissory note with the remark "Rec'd Payment" in the margin, and the date of the receipt. This was not the only loan from rich Philip B. Coles that Aaron Aaron had enjoyed. He had taken as much as twenty-five hundred dollars and as little as a hundred and fifty. The record filled one side of the card and two-thirds of the second side of it.

The other cards were similar. There were fully a hundred and fifty of them, some with only a single notation, the others with several. Sometimes there were two or more cards under a single name, men who borrowed month after month, paying back desperately, still falling in debt, eaten by interest costs, and after several was the curt comment: "Dead, no estate." Or else: "Dead, estate paid in full."

"I sort of can see 'em," said Bill Roan, cocking his head back so that his Adam's apple stood out like the knuckles of a clenched fist. "I sort of can see 'em . . . farmers, I mean, with families . . . waiting out there under the window to see will Philip B. Coles let 'em come up here and beg for more money. He sat up her like God in a cloud."

"Or a hawk on a nest," said Tenner.

"What I notice," said Buck, "is that pretty near every-one of these people paid up in full, except the ones that death got first. He was a kind of a lucky banker, if he didn't take no losses. Didn't he have any loans outstanding when he died, Tenner?"

"Of course he did," said Tenner. "You take a man that's gorged with blood money all the time, d'you think he stops feeding on it? No, he wants more and more. And that's the way with Philip B. Coles. He had twenty or thirty more accounts that weren't settled. Twenty or thirty more. And some bigger than the rest!"

He laughed again. He lighted a cigarette with hands that shook with pleasure. The cigarette began to burn all up one side.

"He's right," said Buck. "Look where the gaps come. Here's Number 72 to Number 75 all missing. Here's 114 gone. How would that come about, Tenner?"

"Why," said Tenner, "wouldn't it come about if the murderer first unlocks the safe with the keys he takes from Philip B. Coles's pocket . . . and then he goes through the cards in the file and takes out the names of every living man whose account is still open?"

"What good would that be to the murderer?" asked Bill Roan.

"Why, brother," said Tenner, "it might have been a whole lot of good. Maybe it was just because he wanted to take the brainwork of Philip B. Coles and turn around and laugh at Philip B. Coles lyin' on the floor. And maybe before he left he took all those cards, twenty or thirty of them, and rattled them before the open eyes of Coles and asked him to look what was happening. And maybe he turned at the door and says to Philip B. Coles: 'Phil, I hate to leave you, and I'm takin' along a quarter of a million in notes together with twenty thousand in hard cash!' "

"A quarter of a million?" demanded Bill Roan. "You mean to say that Coles had loaned out a whole ocean of money like that?"

"That was the turn-over," said Tenner. "The bank says it must of been over a quarter of a million. The bank knew what funds he was circulating, though it didn't have his list of investments. Stocks and bonds was mighty little in the life of Philip B. Coles. Blood was what he wanted . . ."

"Mr. Murderer," said Bill Roan, "he slicks out with twenty thousand dollars and the account of every livin' dollar that still was owing to Coles. How can he use those cards, though?"

Tenner laughed: "He could drop around and give some of the debtors a glimpse of the cards and tell them that he'd settle for three-quarters, or even half. Otherwise, he turns the cards back to the Coles estate—and the estate can collect as good as ever Philip Coles could."

Tenner grew suddenly weary. He leaned a hand against the side of the door.

"Well," he said, "if you boys have seen what you want . . ."

They went back to their horses, turned for a look at the blank face of the house, and then jogged the mustangs slowly down the hill.

"Murder—and one of two people done it," said Buck. "Tenner done it out of hating Coles; or Blondy done it to get an easy living."

"Blondy?" exclaimed Bill Roan. "He never done it in a thousand years!"

"Didn't he, though?" asked Buck. "I tell you what— Blondy was too doggone lazy and dreamy to want to spend his life working all the time. They took and built him up here in Jasper till he felt his oats right through his system. The town thinks that he done it; half the town, anyway."

They came out from the shadows of the trees into the white heat of the open. A horse had just galloped that way before them. The dust stayed in the windless air, not in a flowing cloud but in hanging tufts of mist.

Someone called out. They saw a pale-faced young man who was waving to stop them. When they drew rein, he came up puffing and sweating. He took off his hat and mopped the red streak of the hatband on his forehead.

"I just happened to see you," he said, "and remembered that Perry Baldwin wanted you. Will you go up to his office and see him? Second and Main Streets."

"What would he want with us for?" asked Buck. "He

knows that we're friends of The Streak. The whole of the town knows that."

"He just asked me to find you," said the secretary. "I only know what he says, not what he thinks."

"We won't go," said Bill Roan to Buck.

"Why not?" asked Buck. "Meeting up with Perry T. Baldwin, that shows we're steppin' right out among them."

That was why they went down to the offices of Perry T. Baldwin. In a few moments they were confronting the mahogany gleam of the Baldwin desk, and feeling the soft of the rug silence their footfalls. Even the spurs seemed to jingle with bells abashed. Baldwin came out from behind his desk and gave them each a good, firm handshake, a good, firm look between the eyes.

He said: "Sit down, boys." And then he went back behind the desk. The glimmer of its polished surface stretched a distance between him and the two cowpunchers. They could feel the dust on their clothes as though it had been dirt on the skin. Half across the sheen of his desk he stretched a powerful arm, the fist clenched.

"Boys," he said, "you're friends of The Streak. Friendship is a thing I honor. The Streak is a man I cannot honor. In my position in Jasper Valley, I have to fight for law and order. In that fight I have to use every weapon that will fit my hand. I want to use the two of you. Will you listen to me?"

"He says will we listen to him," said Bill Roan, translating.

Buck crossed his legs. "Yeah. I heard him," he said "What would you want to say, Mr. Baldwin? Sure, we're friends of The Streak. I mean, we been and worked alongside of him for a good stretch. But he ain't a blood-brother or anything like that."

"He'd trust you, wouldn't he?"

"I kind of guess that he would," said Bill Roan, looking hard at Buck.

"Boys," said Baldwin, "I want to pay you out of my own pocket to do a good turn for law and order. How much would you want?"

"You mean?" said Buck.

"For The Streak," said Baldwin.

"He means, what will we take for turning in The Streak," said Bill Roan.

"I guess about a thousand dollars would suit me," said Buck.

"A thousand dollars!" exclaimed Baldwin, throwing up his hands.

"I hate like the devil to do it," said Bill Roan, "even for a thousand. We get a split on the five thousand reward, too?"

"You get a split on that, too."

"The way it looks to me," said Buck, "if we don't turn The Streak over, somebody else will do it. We can use the money as good as the next man; we could lump in together, Bill, and make a fine start at ranching in a small way."

"We could," said Bill, rubbing some painful wrinkles out of his forehead.

"So that's that," said Buck. "A thousand apiece and a cut in the reward money."

"I'll pay you an advance to bind the bargain," said Baldwin, after looking down a moment into his own mind to consider the price. "I'm not a haggler. I accept the terms and will give you a hundred apiece right now."

"Wait till we deliver the goods," answered Bill Roan. "That's the best way of doing business, ain't it?"

"It *is* the best way," agreed Baldwin, heartily. "And now, my friends, I want to ask you, point blank, if you feel a reasonable confidence that you will be able to reach The Streak quickly?"

"Yeah. I got a reasonable confidence that we can," said Bill Roan. "What I'd like to ask is why you're so burned up to do in The Streak. Why should *you* want to spend so much money on him?"

"Boys, I don't mind telling you," said Baldwin, shaking his head gravely, "that Philip B. Coles was a man I respected, admired in some ways, and deeply pitied. To leave his murder unrevenged would be to me a lasting cause for self-condemnation. Can you understand my viewpoint?"

"No private grudge, eh?" asked Buck.

"Why no," said Baldwin. "I suppose you've heard about the fiasco of the other night? Of course you have. Because of course I remember seeing you in the house. Well, it's not that failure that stimulates me to greater efforts now. Once again The Streak showed himself to be what he is: a merciless gunman. But I knew that of him before. The truth is that my investments in Jasper Valley are so large that I cannot afford to see unpleasant news coming out from it—news of murder, and outrage. It will bar incoming capital, incoming laborers, incoming people of the best sort, and attract the attention of other scoundrels and murderers throughout the country. *That* is why I have determined to put The Streak beyond the chance to injure Jasper Valley again."

"That sounds right and reasonable," agreed Bill Roan. "When are you ready to act? Now?"

"Why not?" asked Bill Roan.

"I'm going to introduce you, then, to a man who will act as the cutting edge of the tool. You two will be the guiding hands, so to speak, but I will give you someone who should be able to take care, with your assistance, of even such a celebrated ruffian as The Streak."

He rose from his desk, crossed to a door, and rapped on it three times. The door noiselessly sagged open a few inches, then drifted wide. A small man stepped onto the threshold.

"Boys," said Perry T. Baldwin, "I want you to make the acquaintance of Calico Charlie. Calico, meet Buck McGuire and Bill Roan. They'll lead you to The Streak."

CHAPTER 13

Surprise for Calico

THEY did not ride through the streets of the town together, of course. Instead, Calico Charlie took his horse and rode out north, then swung around and reached the rendezvous on the trail near the main western road. The horse of Calico Charlie was in utter contrast to his brilliant clothes. It was a lumpheaded mustang with a roached back and narrow quarters and a ratty tail. He was as ewe-necked as a cow. But he had four good legs under him, and he could gallop all day long under the light burden of Calico Charlie.

At the stable where Calico went for the horse, it was led out to him by a huge Negro whose breath was sweetened by rum that had reddened his eyes, also. He was a great lump of India rubber, this black man; his face was a round lump with the features thumbed into it with a childish lack of art or care. One could never tell to which side his mouth would slip and spill when he talked. His nose was hardly seen; it was merely a pair of flaring nostrils.

Calico said: "Shine, you're drunk."

"Me, Mr. Calico?" said Shine. "I ain't drunk, sir. I just sort of washed out my throat, sir. Maybe a couple of drops trickled down my throat, but that's all. Not more than a couple of drops, sir."

Calico showed the pink of his smile above his clean white fore-teeth. He shook his riding quirt and stripped the lash thoughtfully through the fingers of his left hand.

Shine trembled.

He said: "I could walk a line, boss. I could walk it on my hands. I ain't had much to drink. The trouble is the size of my mouth. It gives the rum a chance to get right onto my breath. It takes quite a good sized drink to get to the roots of my tongue, Mr. Calico. That's the God's truth, sir."

"You dog!" said Calico, and mounted.

Shine clung to the bridle. "You ain't leaving me, boss, are you?" he asked.

Calico raised his quirt but Shine leaped yards and yards away, and his master rode out silently into the sunshine.

That was the start of the ride that brought Calico to the rendezvous, where he saw Bill Roan and Buck Mc-Guire issue out of the tall brush and wave a greeting.

He skirted away from that brush. He had had word that these men had been bought by Perry T. Baldwin, but he could not be sure of anything, in this life. And Buck McGuire looked like a fighting bulldog, and Bill Roan was like a long, lean greyhound. Good or bad, both were men.

At a little distance from the brush, the pair joined Calico.

"You know where The Streak is?" asked Calico.

"He's at the Layden place," said Buck.

"No," said Calico.

"What you mean by no?" asked Bill Roan. "That's where he is."

"No," said Calico. "Nobody would be that much of a fool."

"I'm telling you the truth," said Buck. "You may call him a fool, and perhaps he is. But after Baldwin and the rest raided the house, The Streak didn't feel that he had to leave and go back to his hideout again, right away. Wherever the crowd would look for him, they wouldn't look at ground they'd just ridden over."

"When did he get there?" asked Calico.

"Right through the posse. It was his horse that he stampeded into the line of picket horses. The whole posse went piling off after the horses, and they sure shot a lot of holes in the air while they were on the way. The Streak came right on into the house. How many of those horses are still on the loose, Calico? You heard Perry T. Baldwin say?"

"Eight," said Calico, smiling.

"And Baldwin has to pay for them?"

"Yes," said Calico, smiling to the pink again.

What he had been told occupied his mind for some time, and very pleasantly, to all apearances.

"Somebody told me," said Bill Roan, "that you have the old guns of Wild Bill Hickok, with the six extra inches on the barrels. But I suppose that's a lot of hokum. People that ain't anything themselves have got to find something to talk about, don't they? You wouldn't be packing around a pair of big rods that size, would you? It'd weigh down your hands too much and you couldn't—"

The hands of Calico jerked up from the reins, slipped under the jacket, and flashed out again. The least, breathless part of a second was all he had needed to make a pair of old single-action Colts gleam in the sunlight. They were huge weapons, long-barrelled.

Both Bill Roan and Buck McGuire stared at the guns with amazement.

"Lemme see one, will you?" asked Buck. Calico smiled his pinkest and pushed the guns up into the spring holsters that suspended them beneath the pits of his arms.

"All the way from Wild Bill to the Tombstone days, the hair trigger and a thumbed gun, and the hammer resting on an empty chamber of course. That was the way they all done, I guess," said Buck.

Calico looked at him with his pale eyes, and said nothing.

"Wild Bill was the greatest of them all," said Bill Roan. "I'll tell you what my grandfather's brother seen. He seen Wild Bill standing a hundred yards from a street sign, and he took out both his guns and turned them loose. Done all his shooting with his right hand, and he kept the left-hand gun pronto and plenty ready. He could fan a gun with his hand so fast that all the noise of the shooting run together, and you couldn't tell the pause when he dropped the right-hand gun and slapped the left hand into his palm. There was an 'O' in the middle of that sign, that day, and when Wild Bill got through with it, there wasn't any wood left inside the loop. He'd shot it clean away, and yet he hadn't scratched the paint of the 'O' itself. What you think about that, Calico?"

"A lie," said Calico.

"He says it sounds like a lie," translated Bill Roan.

"He didn't say that it sounded like anything," answered Buck. "He said that it *is* a lie."

"Well," said Bill Roan, "that might make trouble between me and some folks, but it never would make trouble between *you* and me, Calico. I'd rather throw a firecracker into a cave full of rattlesnakes and then jump in after it had exploded than get into a war dance with you, Calico. You remember Sad Steve Wilson?"

"Yes," said Calico.

They were riding through a country of rolling green patched with round-head groves of trees. The heat was so great that they followed a rather weaving course, taking advantage of every chance to dip into the cool of the shadows and let the dimness flow over them for a moment, as grateful to the skin as flowing water.

And they were so busy with their talk that not even Calico noticed a barelegged boy who drifted to the rear on a piebald pony. To be sure, he kept well down in the hollows and never showed himself against the sky except for a moment, unavoidably.

Bill Roan went on: "Sad used to tell me a lot about you, Calico. He only had the half of a right hand, when I knew him, and he used to tell me how you bit off the other half with a bullet. *He* said—Sad did—that you socked that bullet into him at that place right on purpose, but I said that nobody could shoot as fast and as straight as all that. Was I right?"

"No," said Calico.

He began to brush some dust off the sleeves of his jacket, and seemed to have forgotten the conversation of the men beside him.

"He says that I'm not right," translated Bill Roan, looking on Buck with troubled eyes.

"He means," said Buck, "that now and then a man can get in a good quick snapshot. He don't mean that people can shoot nowadays the way that they used to when the old timers were stepping high. Maybe the liquor we drink ain't so good for the nerves. Maybe we take to beer too much. Maybe prohibition done something to all of us. But we ain't the same as the old timers."

Two guns flashed like fine blue fire into the hands of Calico. The left gun he held a bit out to the side. The right gun he carried just above the height of the pommel of his saddle and flicked the hammer so rapidly with his thumb that the five shots blended in one thunder-roll. The empty revolver went into his left palm, the other gun into his right, and with hardly a pause the second group of shots roared out.

The head of a fence post twenty yards away swayed to the side and fell as far as the top strand of the barbed wire would permit it to drop. The post had been cut clean through by the spray of lead, and the top of the post now swayed up and down slowly, on the suspending strand of wire.

The smell of burned gunpowder stained the air.

Tall Bill Roan, well bent over his saddle, his face twisted all to one side, sighted down a revolver at Calico.

"Stick up those hands!" said Bill Roan. "Stick up your

hands and keep 'em stuck right to the sky; you poison dog, if you move, I'm gonna split your wishbone for you!"

Calico slowly raised his hands, the guns in them.

"Drop those guns!" said Bill Roan.

The pale, patiently steady eyes of Calico dwelt upon Bill Roan. The tension of Bill was so great that the high-light on the muzzle of his Colt trembled rapidly. Calico dropped both his guns.

And the sleeve of the jacket, slipping down a little, re-vealed the glitter of a jeweled wrist watch, stretched by a platinum elastic band around the narrow bones of the arm.

"Now fan him, Buck," said Bill Roan.

Calico licked his lips and kept smiling. He clasped his raised hands together and continued to stare at Bill Roan.

"Look somewheres else, damn you," said Bill Roan. "You make me feel like the buzzards had already started to feed on me, and was beginning on the eyes."

Calico, licking his lips again, turned his head a little and considered the horizon. Out of it a bare-legged boy was galloping a piebald horse at great speed.

He waved his hand; he began to shout joyously from the distance.

"It's that kid Jimmy," said Buck, "and he's got the look of being on our side of things."

CHAPTER 14

Calico's Red Face

THE extravagant happiness of Jimmy subsided a little when he brought it closer to the dignity of grown men. But still he was silently bursting when he drew up on his piebald pony.

"Hello, Mr. McGuire, Mr. Roan. When I seen you first. I almost thought you was with . . . that . . ."

Instead of a word, he pointed at little Calico Charlie.

"How long you been watching us?" asked Bill Roan.

"Ever since I seen Calico start out of Jasper."

"Know where he was going?"

"Why would Perry T. Baldwin of sent for him except that The Streak was in his mind?"

"You got a brain in the old head," said Bill Roan.

"What kind of a skunk is this," demanded Buck, "that carries perfume around with him?"

Buck had his hands full of a platinum cigarette lighter, some colored silk handkerchiefs delicate as wisps of sunset mist, a platinum cigarette case, a wallet of red morocco, tooled exquisitely with gold leaf, and a sheaf of letters. Last of all there was a small flask made of clouded glass.

"Perfume!" said Buck, holding up the vial.

"Well, doggone if my back legs don't ache!" said Jimmy, staring. "You wouldn't go and mean that, Mr. McGuire, would you?"

"Come and try a whiff of it, kid," said Buck McGuire, and he stuck out his chin as he grinned at Jimmy, who approached the vial gingerly.

"Put your arms down and cross your wrists behind your back, Calico," commanded Bill Roan. "Buck, you use that double half-hitch on him. Got some twine? Lay on the hitches good and tight. There's still poison in the teeth of this snake and we don't even wanta get scratched by him."

Jimmy, having sniffed at the contents of the bottle, thrust it away from him at long arm's reach.

"Here. You take it. It smells worse than a party all full of girls. It smells worse than a funeral, or Easter in church. It smells worse than anything!"

"Come on along, Calico," said Bill Roan, when the wrists of Calico Charlie had been firmly lashed behind his back. "Tie the rope of that mustang to your saddle, Buck."

"You mind telling me where you're going?" asked Jimmy. "Might I come?"

"You might not," said Bill Roan.

"I'd like to see the fight," said Jimmy.

"What fight?" asked Bill Roan.

"When him and The Streak stand up to each other."

"He says that him and The Streak are gunna stand up to each other," translated Bill Roan.

"Does he?" murmured Buck, looking with an eye of agony towards his partner.

"Why should they stand up to each other?" asked Bill Roan. "Ain't we got Calico Charlie right in hand?"

"Oh, I see what you mean," answered Jimmy. "You think that a man like The Streak would just pull out a gun and shoot him dead. But he ain't gunna."

"You know, do you?"

"Yes," said Jimmy. "You may be pretty old friends of his, but The Streak and me are kind of thick. I tell you what he went and done."

"Go on, Jimmy."

"He put me up on Rocket, and he gentled Rocket and made him walk along right easy and steady, for a minute. Him and me are the only two that ever sat on the back of Rocket without being pitched right onto the hard rim of Kingdom Come in no time at all."

"Well, you seem to know The Streak pretty good, so what will *he* do with Calico?"

"That's easy," answered Jimmy. "He'll cut the cord off his wrists, and give him a chance to rub his arms till the circulation comes back into them good. Then he'll give him a drink or maybe something to eat."

The horses went on at a walk drifting the group slowly over the rolling green of the fields. Far away they could hear, small as distant cow-bells, the chattering of the work that progressed on Perry T. Baldwin's estate for the building of the great railroad station that was to bring the Twentieth Century to Jasper Valley.

"You think that The Streak will give Calico a sort of a party, do you?" asked Buck of the boy.

"Kind of," said Jimmy, confidently. "And afterwards he'll say 'Well, Calico, I suppose it's about time to get down to business. Here we are five paces away. I've just put your favorite guns where you can use them. Now fill your hands and we'll play it out!'"

The last words, Jimmy crowed out in an ecstasy, at the top of his voice.

He added, in lower tones: "I can kind of see it—The Streak just waiting to the last hundredth of a second before he shoots—and Calico going down with his gun still talking. And The Streak he only shoots that once, because

he wouldn't sink lead into a dying man, and he just lifts
the muzzle of his gun a little and waits, sort of with one
foot in advance. And then Calico hits the ground; and he
dies, kicking out his heels, and whanging the ground with
his hands, and not breathing good."

"How you like that, Calico?" asked Bill Roan.

Calico covered his buck teeth with difficulty and moistened his lips. He resumed his smiling in silence.

They had reached a turn of the dim trail where it
branched, and as they kept along the left hand side, Jimmy sang out: "But you're gunna take him to The Streak,
ain't you?"

"We had an idea like that, maybe," admitted Bill Roan.

"But he ain't up there," said Jimmy.

"Where is he, then?" demanded Buck.

"Why—don't you know yet?"

"No. Where else would he be except—"

"And he ain't even told you?" demanded Jimmy, his
eyes popping out.

"Aw, go on and tell us where he is, if you know," said
Bill Roan.

"I dunno," said Jimmy. "You *seem* like old friends.
You *act* like old friends. But how could I tell that he'd
want to trust you with everything he trusts me?"

"You beat hell out of anything I ever heard of," said
Buck, angrily. "Go on and show us the way, will you?"

Jimmy considered, sweating with anxiety. The horses
began to nibble grass.

"Well, I'll tell you what I'll do," he said. "You start
along up this right hand trail, and keep right on going,
not too fast. I'll gallop on ahead and see what The Streak
wants to do. And I'll come and meet you on the trail before you been gone half an hour. Is that all right?"

Bill Roan swore and nodded and waved his hand, so
the piebald instantly was away at full gallop and quickly
disappeared around the edge of a grove of trees. The
other three followed along the trail at a walk or a dogtrot.

"Leave us see what's inside those letters you took from
Calico," said Bill Roan.

"That's a good idea," agreed Buck.

"No!" said Calico.

"Look at him," observed Bill Roan. "He's turned clean mad. Got a lot more color in his face, too."

"If you look at those letters—" said Calico.

"He's all burned up," said Bill Roan. "Look here, Calico. I thought you were the bird that never batted an eye, no matter how bad the going got for you? I thought you were the hard-boiled gent that never cared a damn whether he went to hell or the cooler place? But you're doggone near to breaking down right now."

"Leave me see," said Buck. "If it's enough to put Calico on the ragged edge. it's enough to hang him by a process of law, whatever that may be."

He opened one of the letters. Calico closed his eyes. A sharp, deep furrow of agony cut into his forehead. And Bill Roan stared at this alteration of expression with a sort of awe.

"Hey, what of we got here?" exclaimed Buck. "Hey, Bill, will you listen to this?" He read aloud: " 'Adored Cecile—' "

"Ah, my God," said Bill Roan, "is it gunna be that kind of dirty stuff?"

"Wait a minute," said Buck. "Get an earful of it! It's kind of thick. Listen!

" 'Adored Cecile, the minute you went out of the room, my heart was following you. It went along up the stairs with you. The creaking of them stairs was a sort of sweet, sad music to my heart. When I heard your door close, I felt as though it had slammed against my face. I felt sick. Forgive me if I said something wrong to you. I haven't been raised like other people and sometimes I don't know what to say. All I was trying to say was that I love you! And then you got angry, and went away. Will you let me come again? Will you say one word? Your unhappy lover, Charlie.' "

"It aint real," said Bill Roan. "You made up a lot of that, Buck, you damn liar."

"How would I make up stuff like that?" asked Buck. "Look at Calico and see."

The face of Calico was deepest crimson that looked like red paint, he was sweating so fast.

"Try another one, and don't let it be a love letter," said Bill Roan.

"No!" breathed Calico.

"You wasn't raised like other people," commented Bill Roan. "Most of us was raised on milk, but you was raised on perfume. That's what made you such a runt—and turned you so sweet. Ain't you ashamed to be alive, for writing a fool letter like that? Who's Cecile, anyway? And how could a gal stand the look of you, anyway? A gal would as soon kiss a cold chisel as run up against those prongs that stick out of your face."

The head of Calico. which hitherto always had been held high, dropped a little. He stared down at the neck of his horse.

"Here comes the kid," said Buck. "He's bringing the news from the king. Hey, Calico, do you want these letters back?"

"Yes," said Calico, suddenly lifting his head.

"Say *please,* damn you!"

"Please," said Calico.

CHAPTER 15

Four Cartridges

JIMMY, coming up at the lope of his piebald horse, announced: "The Streak says to bring you right on. You know what he was doing? He was sleeping, Mr. Roan. Just lying asleep in the straw, and all of this fuss going on outside. You know what he said when I told him that you had Calico? He said: 'Well, who's Calico?' That's a funny one, ain't it? Imagine nobody not knowing him!"

In the meantime, he led the way through the tangle of trees which presently grew much smaller in size, but even more dense. It was a typical second-growth denseness of lodge pole pines such as spring up to occupy the places of the larger trees after fire or any other forest disaster.

"What you taking us to?" demanded Bill Roan.

"You gunna see in a minute," said Jimmy. "Nobody but The Streak ever would have found out a place like this,

I can tell you. But look at here. Right there among the trees. You see that black with the weeds and the trees growing up over it? That's where the Simons's house used to stand before it burned down thirty years ago. You see where the lodge poles are growing? Everything up to the big trees—you can see where they begin—used to be the clearing, and the Simons's house used to stand before it burned down and everything else was left. Even a right good barn like this!"

They could make it out—a good, upstanding barn that might have mowed away fifty or sixty tons of loose hay in the old days. The trees fenced it in, even pressed against the side of it. No trail appeared through that dense growth of the lodge pole pines. It was necessary to weave and press through the shouldering trees until the three riders came behind Jimmy to the side of the barn.

Here several of the trees had been felled, and so recently that the stumps were white and still seemed to be sweating out the sap of their life. In front of this small clearing appeared not the sliding door of the barn but a small door. And on this door Jimmy knocked. He stepped back after knocking, and his face was ashine.

He whispered: "You'll hear him sing out your own selves, in just a minute!"

And, immediately, the cheerful voice of Blondy called: "Coming! Coming!"

As they dismounted, Buck helping the prisoner down from his horse, the door of the barn was pushed open, and Blondy stood at the threshold with the dimness of the barn behind him, the dark of the shadow ruled with lines of gold where the sun shone through small cracks in the old building.

Blondy said: "Hey, Buck! Hey, Bill! Been picking up a new friend? How are you, Calico? You don't have to keep his hands tied, do you?"

"Do you have to keep his hands tied, Buck?" asked Bill Roan.

"Sure I don't," said Buck. "Leave his hands free, Blondy. Maybe I better give him back the guns we borrowed off him, too."

He showed the two ponderous revolvers to Blondy.

"Look at 'em!" said Blondy, laughing.

"You ought to keep a pack mule just for packing along a pair of cannon like that. Come on in, everybody. Jimmy, maybe you're not old enough for this man's church?"

Jimmy took a great breath. "Maybe not," he said. "But—I'd sure like to see him drop."

"I'll be seeing you, Jim," said Blondy. "How does the cow come along, these days?"

"She's off her feed," answered Jimmy. "The air in Jasper Valley these days is kind of strong for her—Well, I better be going. So long, everybody."

He backed up towards his piebald, slowly, but since no one invited him to remain, he mounted and walked the horse off through the lodge pole pines. His last backward glance showed the four men disappearing into the shadows of the barn.

Once inside, it was not as dark a place as the first shadowy look of it promised. A double line of stalls ran down the sides of the barn, but the mangers had fallen down in several places and Blondy led both men and horses right into the mow itself.

At one end appeared two or three feet of hay which had turned paler than the most sun-faded straw in the course of the years. Where the ground was bare, Blondy had grouped his few comforts around one of the big square posts that held up the roof high overhead.

His blankets, rolled down on a sloping mattress of the old hay, were only a step or two from the post, on which hung his coat and sombrero, a slicker, and some odds and ends of clothing. A section of overturned manger provided a bench.

"How's it when it rains in here?" asked Buck.

"It's pretty good," said Blondy. "They built this barn out of clean timber; there's hardly a knothole in the place and even when the rain comes down on the roof like galloping horses, not enough beats through the cracks to more than make the air feel a little wet."

"It's not a bad hangout," said Bill Roan. "For a bird that hates working, this is all right. It's a peg above one of Perry and Applethwaite's shacks, I'd say."

"Sure it is," answered Blondy. "Now, what's what? Sit

down, everybody. Sit down, Calico. Want me to make you a cigarette?"

Calico Charlie said nothing, so Blondy rolled a cigarette out of wheatstraw papers and Bull Durham. He held the flap of the paper for Calico to lick, and then smoothed down the edge, put the smoke in Calico's mouth, and lighted it.

"Maybe you kind of take to him, Blondy," said Bill Roan. "Maybe you kind of like the looks of Calico?"

"Jimmy's been telling me about him," said Blondy, watching Calico smoke, the short upper lip of the gunman pulling down with difficulty over his long front teeth. "I suppose he's raised his share of hell. But what are we going to do?"

Ceaselessly, with his pale eyes, Calico Charlie watched Blondy, standing big before him, with a line of sunlight burning like a fire deep in his hair.

"He says what are we going to do?" translated Bill Roan to Buck.

"How could he be askin'?" demanded Buck McGuire. "We're gunna turn Calico loose and give him back his guns and see that he's got plenty of spendin' money in his pocket. That's what we're gunna do, naturally."

"Stop kidding me, Buck, and tell me the straight of it," said Blondy. "My idea is, Calico will give us his promise to leave Jasper Valley and stay away forever. Then we can turn him loose."

"His idea is that we turn him loose—" began Bill Roan. And then he broke off to add: "Ah, hell!"

At this touch of bitter ridicule, the pale eyes of Calico burned extremely bright, and glanced from Blondy to Bill Roan, and back again.

"But why not?" asked Blondy, making an outward gesture with both hands.

"Why not?" said Bill Roan, his voice thick with gloom. "Why not? Why, hell! Your idea being that we trust Calico and believe his word? Hey, Calico, Billy Weston trusted your word, didn't he? Answer up, you damned Gila monster!"

Calico Charlie, in place of answering, spat out his finished cigarette and put his foot on the butt. He removed his foot and regarded the thin wisp of fumes that rose. He said nothing.

Buck McGuire said: "Listen, Blondy. Billy Weston and Calico used to be partners. Calico turned on him, one day, shot him up, left him for dead. Billy crawled a mile, got help, had himself carried to the jail. He promised to confess everything. But before he talked, by the time he was nearly well, this Calico Charlie managed to get word to him that everything was a mistake. Matter of fact, he loved Billy like a brother.

"Anyway, Billy believed him, double-crossed the sheriff, refused testimony, and left the jail bound straight for Calico Charlie. Nobody saw him alive again. But they found his body staked out on the ground and the lids had been cut off his eyes. And his mouth was still gaped open from the scream he was in the middle of when he died. The sun had cooked the eyes right out of his head. No proof against Calico. There never *is* any proof against Calico.

"Nobody could say that he sat on a rock and watched and listened to Billy Weston. Nobody could *prove* it, anyway. But that's what comes of trusting Calico."

Blondy, when he had heard, went a step closer to Calico and leaned over. He put his hands on his knees so that his face would be nearer to a level, and so stared long, long into the eyes of Calico Charlie. Afterwards he straightened slowly, silently, and a shudder went through him, visibly.

"All right," said Buck. "Now you know something about him. What you say we're to do with him?"

"I don't know," said Blondy.

"He's got to die," answered Bill Roan. "If he ever got away from us, alive, we'd be half dead and half rotten the minute he was free."

Calico Charlie drifted his pale eyes and his automatic smile from one to the other, curiously.

"How'll he die?" asked Blondy, staring.

"We'll draw lots," said Bill Roan. "Here's a good place for him. Nobody knows this hangout of yours, Blondy. We're going to plant Calico here under the ground and leave him be. That's all there is to it."

"You mean murder?' asked Blondy.

"Murder? I mean justice!'" said Bill Roan. "I knew Billy Weston. He was a pretty good kid till Calico poisoned him and showed him the easy way. There's a dozen more to add up against Calico, but Billy Weston is enough. There ain't any revenge in this. We're not staking Calico out in the sun with the lids carved off his eyes. We're simply giving him a ticket to hell on the fast express."

"He don't like it," said Bill Roan to Buck.

"He never was nothing but a damn fool kid," said Buck. "He don't understand. Change the subject a minute and talk about something else. Let Calico know just how dangerous the kid is. Let Calico know the whole story. He comes here to Jasper Valley to pick up some hard cash and get a pile more famous. Murder by request. That was gunna be his job, here. You tell him, Bill."

"Shall I tell you, Calico? Shall I tell you the facts about Blondy—the kid you all call The Streak?"

Calico sat up straight. He said one sudden, eager word: "Yes!"

"Go on, Blondy," said Buck. "This sucker wants to know what kind of maneater you really are. You tell him how many bullets you really fired since you reached Jasper Valley."

"One," said Blondy, smiling a little.

Calico, his eyes narrowed, shook his head.

"Yeah, Calico," said Blondy. "Only one. If you'd filled me full of lead, you'd of been doing nothing much. Look here—the gun I pack is always empty."

He broke open his Colt and showed the empty chambers, explaining: "I've got a lot of chances to get into a jam, here in the valley. I might be scared into filling my hand and damaging a lot of property some time. So I keep it cool and light and empty."

He closed the gun and slid it into its holster again.

But Calico still shook his head.

"He don't believe you, kid," said Bill Roan.

"I'll prove it," answered Blondy.

He went to the old slicker that hung by a peg from the post and turned out one of the pockets. The bullets that fell into his hand he carried toward Calico.

"Look here," he said. "The old gun happened to be full when I rode over the hills and the fracas of that holdup

of the bus scared the life out of me. I fired one shot.
That's the only one I used. The rest of 'em are here in my
hand."

Calico shook his head again. "Four," he said.

"What's Calico mean?" asked Bill Roan.

He grabbed the hand of Blondy and pulled the fingers
open. There were only four cartridges inside the palm.

CHAPTER 16

Blondy's Lie

"WELL?" said Bill Roan, when a grim moment of pause
had followed. "Why don't you say something, kid? Where's
the fifth of 'em?"

"Why, I don't know," said Blondy, frowning. "There
have to be five."

He looked uncertainly about him, went back to the
slicker, and examined the canvas pocket again.

There was a faint, hushing sound. That was Calico
Charlie, laughing.

"Coles!" he said.

"Bah!" exclaimed Blondy. "Coles? I know what you
mean. I used one on Philip B. Coles, too. Is that the idea?"

"Well?" demanded Buck, his face puckered, his jaw
thrust out.

"Well," said Blondy, "I'll tell you the facts."

He cleared his throat. "They're so silly," he said, "that
I hate to tell them. But the truth is that my nerves have
been getting pretty well filed down, recently. And the
other night, when the thunderstorm blew over, the lightning cracked right over my head and threw a terrible scare
into me. I got jumpy and loaded the old gun again. Shows
that I never ought to pack a loaded gun around with me.
I lighted the lamp, there, and it kept swaying a little
from the nail, and the shadows kept waving and jumping
through the room. There was another crash of the old
thunder. It sounded as though boards were being ripped
right off the side of the barn. Wouldn't take much to

do that, you know. I thought, suddenly, that they were breaking in through the wall behind me, and they'd shoot me down by the light of my own lamp.

"You know how things like that work in you. You think everything over in the wink of an eye. I spun around with that fool of a gun in my hand and let her blaze. Then of course I saw that there wasn't anything in the barn. I was alone. Everything was all right. I felt like a fool."

"What did you do with the empty shell?" demanded Buck, his face still rigid with suspicion.

"I broke the gun open right away," said Blondy, "and took the cartridges out. You know. Shooting at a shadow, that way, convinced me that I shouldn't be packing a loaded Colt any longer. I'd known that before. I put the bullets back into a pocket of the slicker."

"Where's the empty shell, then?" demanded Buck, again.

"Why, naturally I dropped that into my coat pocket and forgot about it till the next time I was riding out. Then I chucked it away, somewhere."

"That sounds reasonable," said Bill Roan.

"Where's the hole in the wall?" demanded Calico Charlie.

Bill Roan and Buck lifted their heads. Calico stood up, also, and moved over towards the wall of the barn, still staring like the others at the roof and the sides of the building. It was true that the old barn had been built of clean lumber. There was not a knot hole, not a single eye of light that sifted down its rays towards them, except for those thin, golden lines of sunshine that seeped through the cracks.

Buck said: "Coles! I kind of knew it from the first. Coles! You killed him."

"What are you talking about?" cried Blondy. "The bullet—I don't know. It might have gone into the ground, or into the hay."

"You know when a gent shoots wild, he always shoots high," said Buck. "You been lying. I can see the lie still workin' in your damned eyes. You murdered Coles, you rat! You been living on dead man's money all this while. Why don't you come out and say it?"

Bill Roan slowly hung his head.

"You're wrong, Buck," said Blondy. "I suppose you've got reason for thinking this way. But my God, because a bullet is gone from my gun, you can't blame Coles on me and—"

Here there was a screeching sound from the side wall of the barn as two of the sun-warped, wide boards were wrenched away, the rusted nails screaming against the wood. They turned to see Calico Charlie dive through the gap into the sunlight. They saw the vast bulk and the deformed, rubbery face of Shine.

The bullet from Bill Roan's gun drilled neatly through the boards as they swung down again, the upper nails still fast and serving as hinges.

"The horses! Mind the horses!" shouted Buck, sprinting for the two swingboards.

He burst through them with Bill Roan at his shoulder. Far ahead of them, they heard the crackling as footfalls sped through the underbrush; then there was silence.

"They'll come back, the murdering two of them," said Buck.

"What have we gone and let happen? What have we gone and done? Let's get out of here, Bill, before they start stalking the barn—and us."

They went back through the small door and found Blondy with the horses.

"Where's your horse?" said Bill Roan. "Climb on that mustang of Calico's and get out of here—the pair of 'em will be coming after us, and what are two like Buck and me against 'em? Move!"

Blondy was already in the saddle on Calico's horse.

They pressed the horse through the second growth pines and out into the open. A brisk gallop put a mile of green rolling ground between them and the barn. Then they drew rein for a moment.

Buck said: "You done fine, Blondy. You beat it for the horses. You didn't run in the wrong direction at all. You got the whole barn between you and trouble. You done it pronto."

"I started for the guns," said Blondy. He pulled out the two long guns of Calico.

And he explained, as he put them away again: "Then

I heard you sing out to mind the horses. And I did what you said. I just remembered then that the two guns were both of them empty."

"You got a brain five years old," said Buck. "But it's old enough for murder."

"Steady, Buck," cautioned Bill Roan.

"Here's where the trail divides," said Buck, "and here's where I leave you, Blondy. I hope I never lay eyes on you again. I'm sorry for every minute I ever spent with you. I'm through. I wash my hands of you. Come on, Bill, and leave him be."

Blondy held out a hand. "Buck," he said, "I'm sorry you feel like this. I don't blame you. It looks rotten."

"You can't talk to me," said Buck. "Bill, come along with me."

"Hold on," said Bill Roan.

"Hold on to what? Hold on to murder? Let's get out of the sight of him and stay out."

"The kid's in a hole, Buck," said Bill Roan.

"He dug it himself. I hope it's deep enough to bury him inside of."

"I can't pull out on him," said Bill Roan.

"Wait!" shouted Buck. "Blondy, you lied about shooting the gun off, back there in the barn, didn't you?"

"Yes, I lied," said Blondy.

"What did become of the fifth bullet, then?"

"I don't know," said Blondy, miserably.

"The hell you don't know!" cried Buck. "You sunk it into the head of Philip B. Coles, like everybody knows you did. Bill, is that enough for you? Are you coming with me, or are you staying with this skunk?"

"I wanta talk to you, Buck," said Bill Roan.

"You can't talk to me, not if you wanta talk about him. Are coming?"

"I can't leave the kid in a hole," said Bill Roan.

"Then to hell with everybody," said Buck, and spurred his horse away at a full gallop.

A grove of trees blotted him suddenly from sight.

Bill Roan said: "Seems like there's been a thunderstorm, or something. The sky looks kind of big and empty, don't it?"

Blondy said nothing.

"Where do we go from here, kid?"

"I don't know."

"If you want to keep your skin whole, you get out of Jasper Valley and keep on traveling, or Calico Charlie will get you sure as hell."

"I know it," answered Blondy. "I'll go to the Layden place and say good-by to Mary. Then I'll go. No reason why you should run yourself into danger. You cut along after Buck. You and Buck are old bunkies."

"Leave you to Calico Charlie?" said Bill Roan. "Seems like the little old Calico Charlie had got his gopher's teeth sunk into me, eating me cold. I can't leave you to him. You and me will stick together till I get you out of the valley. Then I'll pick up Buck's trail back to the ranch."

They dog-trotted their horses slowly over the grass that grew small in the center of the trail.

"The trouble with Buck is he gets mad too easy," said Bill Roan. "There ain't anything wrong with Buck, except he gets mad too easy. That's the trouble with him. . . . You don't wanta go and tell a lie to an old chum like Buck, Blondy. You oughta know that."

"I was sort of cornered," said Blondy. "I didn't know what to say. But I still don't know what become of that bullet."

"That's all right," said Bill Roan.

"Bill, listen to me!" exclaimed Blondy.

"I'm listening, kid."

"*You* haven't got it in your head that Buck's right?"

"That's all right," said Bill Roan.

He glanced back over his shoulder. Nothing followed them except the cloud shadows that swept across the grass.

Blondy, staring at his companion, regardless of the horse that carried him, bounced a bit in the saddle.

"You ain't got much of a seat on a horse, kid, have you?" remarked Bill Roan.

"Bill, listen to me!" begged Blondy.

"Yeah, and I'm listening, Blondy."

"I mean about Philip B. Coles. I mean, getting into his room and then, like a murdering coward, shooting him down like that. You don't think that I really did all that, do you?"

"That's all right," said Bill Roan, and looked far off towards the horizon.

Blondy said no more. They kept their horses jogging side by side. After a while, the squeaking of the saddle leather seemed to grow louder and louder; and you could hear the jouncing, squeaking noise of the inwards of the horses.

CHAPTER 17

The Streak's Departure

JUST before they got to the Layden place, Jimmy burst out at them on his piebald pony. He came up at a dead gallop and reined in beside his hero.

"What happened, Streak?" he whispered.

"Oh, nothing," answered Blondy.

"Is Calico dead?" gasped Jimmy.

"No, Calico's all right," said Blondy.

"You didn't kill him? You just fought and—then you let him go? You just took his horse and maybe his guns and then you turned him loose? I *knew* it'd be something like that!" said Jimmy.

He began to laugh with happiness.

"My Lord," said Jimmy, "won't Calico be eating out his heart, now? . . . How'd it happen, Streak? What you do to him? Just shoot the gun out of his hand, maybe? Or what?"

"You go on along home, Jimmy, will you?" asked Blondy.

Jimmy was still laughing. Joy kept him jumping in the saddle.

"I *wish* I'd been there to see," said Jimmy. "Well, so long, Streak. So long, Mr. Roan."

He went off at a dead gallop.

"He'll have that news all over Jasper in five minutes," said Bill Roan.

"I don't care what's all over Jasper," said Blondy.

They turned up the driveway of the Layden place and

checked their horses before the hitching rack. The Layden automobile with its two crumpled front fenders stood near, and the horse of Calico kept stretching out its head and snuffing at the monster, as though it scented the life of the machine.

"Harry's home, too," said Blondy. "That makes it worse."

They got up to the veranda but before they reached that front door they were stopped by a voice that was lowered but whose words came with a dreadful distinctness to their ears.

It was Buck McGuire, saying: "He lied to Bill Roan and me. He stood and lied. I seen him turn green. He's the one that murdered Philip B. Coles. It was as good as hearing him confess. It was worse. Lemme tell you, it ain't easy to say. Bill Roan and me loved the kid. There never was a better partner than Blondy before he turned into The Streak—the Yellow Streak."

Bill Roan and Blondy, motionless at the door, stared at one another. The voice of Buck McGuire had ended, and his footfall came down the hallway out of the adjoining room.

He pushed the screen door open and stood with his feet braced well apart, eying Blondy and ready to take the consequences of what he knew had been overheard. Blondy said nothing at all.

Buck snarled: "I'd rather see her married to a bush-tailed coyote that steals chickens and sucks eggs."

Blondy pulled the door open and stepped into the hallway. He did not let the screen slam behind him but eased it home softly. The hallway seemed bigger than ever. The heavy beams of its ceiling were painted white and the grapes—grapes painted and shining white like the beams that crushed down upon them.

The stairway rose with a grand sweep leading up, it seemed to Blondy, to peace and eternal happiness.

When he got to the door of the sitting room he saw Mary Layden sitting in the big chair by the western window, still looking at the images which Buck had put before her eyes.

She said: "Hello, Jim!" and gave him her smile as usual, but it went out suddenly and left an empty blankness. He felt that he had only dreamed she smiled at him. Her head was a little bent, and she kept looking away from him out the window. It framed trees with the sun glittering on them, and a summerhouse of latticework that stood on a little knoll in the garden. Some of the lattice was broken.

Blondy could see the greenery that over-ran the little house dripping down into the interior. That was where she must have played as a child, running in and out, making of it, by turns, a castle, a church, the palace of a king. He looked beyond the garden to two big green hills with a flash of water running between them, and the blue valley of the sky pouring away beyond.

"I know what Buck's been saying," said Blondy. "I've come to say good-by."

"Good-by, Jim," said Mary, still looking out over the garden.

He dropped to a knee in front of her; even then it was rather hard to see her face because she kept it inclined a little. He took her hands. They were always brown and strong and quick, the sort of hands that could throw a rope or use a rifle or saddle a horse almost as well as a man; but now they were cold. The strength had gone out of them. He took the hand that had her grandmother's ring on it and kissed it over the knuckles. His lips pressed the knuckles in. The life was all broken out of them.

He said: "Do you hate to have me touch you, Mary?"

"No," she said. "I like it."

She put her other hand on his head, pushing the fingers slowly through the soft of his hair, but nothing could withdraw her eyes from the vast abstraction which she was beholding in the blue valley of the sky.

"You believe Buck," said Blondy.

She said nothing. Her hand kept moving quietly over his head like the touch of a blind person who wants to envision something.

"All right," said Blondy. "You've got to believe him. I'm going to love you to the last minute. I'm going to love you more and more. Anyway, I'm not worthy to be touching your hand; and I hope some day you find happiness and a man who—"

Here he could not speak any more. He stood up and

waited a moment, hoping that she would look at him. She had not looked once away from the window but just kept there staring at the picture which Buck had painted in the sky.

Then Blondy knew that it would be best for him to get out of the room before she *did* look up. If he stood there, perhaps he would draw her glance around to him. Perhaps the pull of his eyes was what was making her begin to tremble. He got softly to the door and closed it behind him.

Harry came suddenly and loudly down the hall. He cried out: *"Hai! Jim! Hai,* old Jim! How's everything, boy? How's—"

Then he came up to Blondy and took him by the two shoulders.

"What's the matter? What's happened?" he asked.

"I'm going away," said Blondy. "I've just said good-by to Mary. You say good-by for me to your father and mother. I couldn't face saying good-by to them."

"What do you mean you're going away?" demanded Harry Layden. "Going away where?"

"Away from Jasper Valley, somewhere."

"Ah, Jim, they've worn you down, have they? They've kept dropping the acid and finally they've eaten the heart out of you. . . . But nobody else in the world would have dared to stay so long and laugh at their manhunt. I'm going with you, Jim. Nothing can pry the two of us apart."

"You stay home," said Blondy.

They had reached the front door, taking small, hesitant steps.

"You mean that you won't let me come along?" said Harry.

"I can't let you come," said Blondy. "You stay here— Mary—"

"Wait a minute, Blondy. You're not going to walk right off like this, are you? You're going to give me a minute, aren't you? I'm sicker than seasickness."

He spied Buck McGuire and Bill Roan and suddenly strode before Blondy through the door and down the veranda steps towards the hitching rack.

"You had something to do with this!" cried Harry

Layden. "You're the pair that's driving The Streak away from us—"

"You're damned right we are," said Buck McGuire.

He pushed out his jaw and made himself uglier than ever. The big hand of Harry Layden flashed out and got a grip inside the loose of Buck's shirt collar. The size of his hand took up all the slack.

His knuckles like hard rock forced the chin of Buck up.

"Back up!" said Buck, his voice half-stifled. "Don't make me start something."

"I gotta mind to take the pair of you and tear you in two!" said Harry. "The minute I laid eyes on you I knew there'd be trouble. I knew that something bad was catching up with The Streak. I've not only got a mind, but I'm going to—"

"Harry, back up," said Blondy.

Instantly, but reluctantly, Harry loosed his hand and it fell away from Buck, who began to finger his bruised throat. Bill Roan pushed away into his clothes something that he had half drawn.

"All I can do is nothing, is that what you mean, Jim?" asked Harry. "You're going away? You're leaving Jasper Valley, and all of us, and Mary?"

Blondy looked back towards the house. The big veranda stretched out like welcoming arms.

"You're sick, too, Jim," said Harry. "You look sick. You can't go away from us."

"I don't know. I don't know how long before I'll see you," said Blondy. "So long, Harry."

Harry caught his hand. He used both of his own big hands on Blondy's.

"All right," said Harry. "I'm a fool to try to keep The Streak in a place where there's murder on the loose and trying to find him. All right. Good-by, Jim. Good-by, old son. Good-by, Jim."

Blondy got on the horse of Calico; Harry Layden turned about sharply and went striding back towards the house with his head down. He stumbled on the veranda steps and knocked a rattling thunder out of them. Then the screen door banged behind him.

The three of them were riding down the driveway.

Buck went a little in advance of the other two, and as they came out onto the main road, Jimmy rushed at them out of a cloud of dust on the piebald horse, now dripping with sweat.

"Hey, Streak!" he shouted. "Calico's in town buying new guns. Everybody knows you got his horse. Now they know that you got his guns, too. Nobody ever heard of anything like that!"

"Here, Jimmy," said The Streak. "You want one of those big guns for a keepsake?"

"One of Calico's guns? One of the ones that used to belong to Wild Bill? Streak, you don't mean you're gunna give *me* this, do you?"

"It's a keepsake, Jimmy."

"You mean I'm gunna remember you by it? What a chance I'd have ever of forgetting you! But what you mean keepsake, Streak. You ain't going away, are you?"

"I guess I am," said Blondy. "I'm saying good-by, Jimmy. You've been the best kid I ever met. You've been the best in the world."

Jimmy slid off his horse as though his legs had turned too weak to keep him in his place on the piebald's back. He held up his hand and turned up his face to The Streak.

"You're going away. You're gunna go away!" said Jimmy. "I didn't ever think it would happen, somehow."

A convulsion began in his stomach and shook and bent his entire body.

Tears began to run down his face, which was hideously distorted. "Mostly I'm not a baby, Streak," he said. "But it's not having had a chance to get ready for it; it sort of socks me when I'm not looking. Good-by, Streak. Would you let me ride a little ways with you?"

"I can't do that," said Blondy.

He rode on, turned in the saddle to look back at the boy. The sun was rolling down the west, puffing out its cheeks with gold.

"Take him by and large," said Blondy, "that's the best kid I ever met in my life. Bill, I've got to branch off, here. I'm not riding on with the two of you."

"Don't you go and be a damn fool," said Bill Roan. "I'm gunna stay with you, kid."

"No, I'm going by myself," said Blondy. "So long, Bill. God bless you. You've been a pal. Good-by, Buck. Go on and shake hands. You did what you thought was the right thing. Maybe it *was* right. Maybe I ought to hate you, but I don't. So long. Good luck."

He rode off through the trees at a lope. Buck Mc-Guire, with a dazed face, continued to stare down at his right hand, as though he could not believe what had happened to it.

CHAPTER 18

Blondy's Courage

THAT ragged old mustang of Calico Charlie's had a nice little dog-trot, and it moved along with its head down, and nodding, and its hoofs just trailing through the dust in the way that a mustang knows how to travel all day long. Blondy was not the best rider in the world, but he sat that dog-trot without stirring in the saddle.

Around him, green islands of trees on the paler green of the grass drifted past, and he looked on them with a hopeless and dim eye.

He hardly guided the mustang at all. It seemed to know the way and went straight on until it came to that brake of lodge-pole pines. Even there it did not hesitate. Having once been crowded through that dense thicket, it pressed forward again. Its flattened ears showed how it hated all riders; the spur scars on its flanks were the symbol that it had learned the wisdom of serving them. So they came to the little side door of the barn.

Blondy dismounted, threw the reins, and walked into the dimness of the interior. It was quite black, after a trip through the brilliance of the outer day, even though the sun was almost down. Blondy found the lantern, lighted it, and went to the post from which his spare clothes were hanging. He began to go through the pockets of everything: the breast pockets of flannel shirts, the hip and side and watch pockets of overalls, the outside, inside, complicated pockets of a cheap old coat.

Finally he paused in his work and rested a hand blindly against the post.

Behind him the voice of Calico Charlie suddenly said: "Just rest a while, kid. Then you can turn around and talk to Calico."

Then someone laughed, in a husky, high-pitched, whining key. That was Shine, of course.

Blondy turned around. He seemed to see nothing except the two of them smiling, the shine of their eyes and of their teeth.

Calico said: "Fan him."

Shine went up to Blondy and took a grip on his flannel shirt at the base of the neck. The vast grasp of his black hand took up all the spare of the shirt and put on a pressure that made breathing hard. He slapped his other hand against the clothes of Blondy.

The slaps were so flat and heavy that they stung right through the cloth and made Blondy seem naked. The first thing that he found was the gun of Calico, the famous old Colt with the extra inches on the barrel.

Calico said: "Any bullets in that old gun, Shine?"

"No, sir," said Shine.

"Give it back to him," said Calico.

Shine gave it back.

He found tobacco, papers, matches, a little twist of a sewing kit that contained, also, twine and buttons of three sizes. There was a wallet containing over a hundred dollars, and a letter.

That was all. There was nothing else.

"What's in the letter?" asked Calico. "Let him go, now. Maybe he's gunna jump the two of us. But that's all right. What's in the letter?"

Shine unfolded it. He began to chuckle and shake his wide shoulders and his head.

"It's a woman, boss," he said.

"Ah?" said Calico. "Give it to me!"

He took the letter and read it aloud, holding the sheet of paper close to the lantern, and closer and closer, as though he found it hard to make out the words.

Dearest Jim:

It doesn't matter when you come, for that matter, Sometimes I think that father is a little worried when I go out into the woods at night with you. But mother isn't at all. I think she trusts you as she'd only be prepared to trust an angel.

What I think is that you shouldn't come so close to the house. If you stood on the top of Cannon Hill, for instance, and simply lighted a match and moved it up and down, I'd see the signal and come as fast as feet will carry me.

But if you keep coming here, before long they'll learn to wait for you.

So much love to my dear Jim.

Mary.

Calico folded the letter.

He went up to Blondy and said: "You never have much trouble with the ladies, I guess?"

Blondy shrugged his shoulders. "I don't know much about them," he said.

"A fellow your size, good looking and all, with a straight pair of lips over his teeth, he wouldn't have any trouble," said Calico.

"I've never been much with the girls," said Blondy.

"You lie," said Calico. "Why don't you quit lying and tell me what you first said to this one when you met her?"

"I don't remember," answered Blondy.

"Ah, you don't remember, don't you? You don't remember how she happened to fall in love with you?"

"No—she simply seemed to care."

"Like you could see how much she cared?"

"Yes. Like that."

"You never had to say nothing?"

"No."

Calico flashed out a gun and struck Blondy with the butt of it. The blow split his scalp and knocked him down on his knees. He started to get up. Calico kicked him in the face and he fell back on his elbows and hands.

The blood was running down from the scalp wound. The warm, salty taste of it was in his mouth. It seemed as though someone were pounding him at the base of the brain. That was from the effect of the kick, which had landed squarely under his chin. Calico had turned into a spinning mast through which a face was vaguely visible.

"Tell him where he stands," said Calico.

Shine came up and sat on his heels before Blondy.

He said: "You took the guns of Calico, brother, and that wasn't very good sense. But then you went and took his horse, and that was worse sense. So you gotta die. But you mind telling me what for you come back here?"

"Nothing," said Blondy.

"Go on and tell me," said Shine.

"I was looking for something, was all."

"You didn't remember Calico and poor old Shine, I guess?"

"I wasn't thinking about you," said Blondy.

"Boss," said Shine, turning his head, "it's a funny thing, but he ain't afraid."

"Could you make him afraid?" asked Calico.

"Me? I could try," said Shine. He put his hand on the shoulder of Blondy and dug his great fingers one by one through the flesh until the hard tips gritted against the bone. It was like a housewife's feeling of a chicken hanging in the market. "I could sure try," said Shine.

Calico kept on walking up and down, silently.

"Will I try?" asked Shine, "Or you want me to take and tie up something on the place that's running blood out of his head?"

"Cook something," said Calico.

He kept on walking up and down, never looking at Blondy, while Shine lighted a small fire inside the bricks that served Blondy as a hearth. The food supply was kept in a little rack of shelves nailed to one side of a manger. The skillet was kept there, also.

Shine found five pounds of ham and some onions and potatoes. He sliced off the outer skin of the ham and then cut it in thin rashers into the skillet. He used a jackknife that was razor sharp. He cut deep, the heavy peelings dropping with audible little crumplings against the floor.

Then he sliced the potatoes small and dropped them into the skillet in turn. He put the skillet over the fire. It warmed. The ham fat began to sizzle. Into the top of the skillet, which now was heaping, he began to slice onions.

The springing oil from the onions squirted up into the face of Shine. It made him squint. He kept licking his lips and squinting. He started stirring up the mess of ham and potatoes and onions all together. After a while, he reached into the sack, pulled out an onion and bit into the thick red, tough outer skin. He bit right in as though the onion were an apple.

After that, he kept making little grunting noises, as though he were clearing his throat; and he kept on spitting out shreds of the outer skin of the onion.

The smoke of the fire rolled up into the rafters. It grew thicker and thicker. It boiled like a pot. It boiled like a pot turned upside down. Blondy, with his head back, watched those vapors boiling.

It was better to keep his head back, anyway, because less of the blood ran down his face. The bleeding diminished by degrees. At first he had thought that he was going to bleed to death; now he knew that he suffered from nothing but a tear of the scalp.

When his head was tilted like that, he could still see Calico walking up and down with that mincing step, but he could not see Shine. He could only hear the clearing of Shine's throat and hear him spitting out the shreds of the tough onion skin.

The smell of the sizzling ham and the frying potatoes and onions enriched the air. He grew very hungry.

Shine had found the coffee pot and the coffee, too. This came to a boil before the frying had ended. The sweet pungency of the coffee passed into the air. It made Blondy hungrier than before.

Calico came over to him and put the muzzle of a gun against his mouth. His lips shrank from the pain of that pressure. The heavy gun muzzle grated right against his teeth. He could taste the iron. He never realized before that iron had a taste. Also, there was a slight, nauseating sense of old oil.

"Why don't you give a damn?" asked Calico. "Where'd you get the new set of guts?"

The steel of the gun barrel had a blue glimmer to it.

That was nothing compared with the pale brightness of the eyes of Calico.

He said nothing. If he tried to speak, he was afraid that the gun would be rammed down his throat. The front sight would tear the devil out of the tender, red flesh. Calico had the look of wanting to do something like that.

With the gun still at his teeth, Blondy began to think of something else. The old weight rolled slowly back upon his heart. The words of the letter repeated themselves, not in the husky guttural of Calico, but in the sweet voice of Mary Layden.

Calico pulled the gun away.

"Yeah. You got something," he said. "I thought maybe it was only a fake. You got something."

CHAPTER 19

Rocket

"Come and get it, boys!" sang out Shine. He began to clap his hands together. "Come on and get it! Come and get it!"

Calico went over by the fire and sat down on his heels. He pulled out a knife and began to pry into the steaming mess in the skillet. Towards Blondy he made one gesture. Shine got up and stood over Blondy.

He began to talk in a loud, thoughtful voice, filled with pauses. Calico was offering part of the food neither to the Negro nor to his captive. He picked up bits of ham on the end of his knife and ate them, cooling them first with his breath. As he smiled over his buck teeth and ate and swallowed, he looked like a deserted little child alone in the night of the world.

Now and then he sipped his coffee. He ate very slowly. The potatoes and the onions he left unheeded. He simply ate of the meat from that huge, heaping skillet. The greasy smell of the food grew rank in the nostrils of Blondy.

It seemed one of the strangest things in the world that

no food was offered to him. You might have thought that this was as far away as Russia, or something like that. But in America, where people are not starving, to eat without offering food all around—that was too much.

Calico sat back from his eating, rolled and lighted a cigarette. Still he was listening to the monologue of Shine.

"There's some rusty old baling wire over there," said Shine. "I could take and twist some of it around the head of The Streak, and pretty soon it would begin to twist down, boss. It would twist down till the skin was sticking out, all full of blood, under the wire, and above it. It would twist down till it broke the skin and the blood run. Then it would go on twisting down till it begun to cut into the bone. I knew a fellow in Atlanta had that done to him.

"I seen the scar. He said he could stand the first part pretty good. Only it made him feel that he was going to be blind forever. His eyes was popping out of his head and he couldn't close the lids of them. His eyes was popping out so far that some of the rust of the wire dropped down into those eyes and still he couldn't wink the lids. But he stood all that all right. But then the skin broke and the wire twisted down into the bone, and then he said that someone started screaming in a terrible kind of a way. And pretty soon he knew that it was himself that was screaming. We could take and try that on The Streak, if you want him to die like that."

"I've gotta find out something. Take and eat," said Calico.

Shine went over to the skillet. He picked it up and held it inside the curve of his left arm as though it were musical and he fed his great mouth again and again. Blondy grew more hungry as he watched.

The grease spread in an increasing circle around the mouth of Shine. It reached down to his chin and almost to his eyes. No matter how much he picked up in his right hand, there was room for it behind the twisting, shapeless, rubbery lips. He took such vast mouthfuls that wrinkles stood out on his face and blinded the eyes.

He ate all the huge portion of food that was still heaped in the skillet—for Calico had taken very little from the mass. With swabbing movements, Shine cleaned up the last of the fried stuff; then he wiped his hands on his trousers, his greasy face on both sleeves, and turned his attention to the coffee. He did not use a cup. Instead, he lifted the entire pot and drank from it. He made pauses in his great draughts to spit out some of the grounds which had strained out against his teeth. Finally the pot was empty.

"That was pretty good," said Shine.

Calico, sitting on his heels, smoking, all this while was eying Blondy. He was reading as in a book, shifting his eyes from side to side, slowly passing from the top to the bottom of his prisoner, and without turning the page beginning at the top again.

"Luck," said Calico. "The Streak ain't nothing. He just had luck."

"Yeah. Sure. Luck," said Shine.

"Go bring that Rocket horse inside here," said Calico.

"You ain't gunna try to ride that big jackrabbit inside here, are you, boss?"

"Go get Rocket for me," said Calico.

"Boss, ain't you gunna finish that little business you got with Mister Streak before you do nothing else?" asked Shine.

"He's gunna see me ride his horse before he feels me take his scalp," said Calico. "Go get me Rocket, and run."

Shine went unwillingy from the barn.

And for a long time, Calico continued his examination of the face and the presence of Blondy.

He pulled back his foot to kick Blondy; but here Rocket came into the barn and made himself the center of attention. He came in rearing, in spite of a torturing twist taken with a rope on his upper lip. He was not very beautiful from certain aspects, but he was devil all through from the look of him. He knocked his rump against the side of the barn in one of his whirlings, and knocked off three big planks without noticing the impact.

Only by degrees did the torture twist begin to subdue him. He stood still, at last, with the red sheen working in his eyes alone.

Shine kept saying: "Oh, you gunna rocket, are you? You gunna be a jumpin' rocket, are you? I'll rocket you— damn you. You pretty near took the shine off of me, damn you. I'm gunna rocket you. I'm gunna make you like rocketing, I am."

He got a saddle on the horse, and then a bridle, though that was a harder job.

Shine said: "You can't ride this horse, boss. He's got the jump-and-catch-its in his hind legs. You can't ride him.

"Nobody can ride him without he's gentled with a club for a while. Nobody can ride him."

"The Streak," said Calico, pointing at Blondy.

"Yeah. Maybe. I've heard about that. I don't know about that. Nobody can ride this man's horse, boss. Don't you go and try."

"Watch The Streak," said Calico, and swung himself up into the saddle.

His legs seemed to stretch out, there was so much cat in his spring, as he bounded up into the saddle on Rocket.

And Rocket stood for a moment, with his forelegs braced and his head thrust forward, and his ears flopping snuffing the air that blew towards him the scent of Blondy.

"He's gunna be a lamb," said Calico laughing.

"Look out!" yelled Shine.

Rocket did not leap into the air when he started fighting. He was not that sort of a battler. Instead, he simply galloped for the nearest of the big posts that held up the roof of the barn. And though he gave his heel a little to the fierce pull which Calico put on the rein, he kept on going towards his goal.

"He's gunna scrape you off!" yelled Shine. "I'm gunna kill that damned horse. Look out, boss!"

He held Blondy by one shoulder and jammed a gun against his back, between the shoulder blades, but he yelled his cautions at Calico.

Very well and nobly Calico maintained, then, the fame of a good horseman. For he leaned out and raked big Rocket from the cheek to the foreleg with a cruelly slashing spur.

But even that did not turn the horse. He was going with such speed that he could lean his body as he got to the post. Calico was already swinging clear when the pommel of the saddle struck the post. The leather covering went off that pommel like the skin off an apple. The steel frame dug into the wood knife and then buckled as the whole saddle ripped off the back of Rocket and tumbled with Calico on the floor of the barn.

Shine plunged to the rescue.

A shrill, snarling voice came out of the wreckage: "Watch The Streak!"

But Blondy was already gone.

Shine was on his feet and well in the lead as he plunged for that gap in the wall of the barn through which Rocket had gone, with Blondy behind him; but little Calico Charlie fairly won the race to that point of vantage.

Where the dim lantern light walked a step from the gap into the thicket of the lodge-pole pines, Calico stopped and held up a hand to halt Shine.

The Negro was whining with each panting breath he drew, a strange little tremor of sound. And before them they could hear the brush crashing, and the voice of Blondy calling, "Rocket! Rocket! Steady, boy! Good boy!"

And then the rhythmical beating of hoofs and no more cries from Blondy.

"Luck. You can't beat luck," said Calico Charlie.

He leaned a hand against the wall of the barn and stared into the path of the lantern light, dimmer than the moonlight that shines through storm-clouds. The trees were barely visible for a single pace.

"Look!" said Calico Charlie. "He ran through that like it was an open road."

He added: "Go see if my horse is still out there."

Shine lunged into the woods. He came back panting more heavily than ever, shaking his head.

"He took time off to catch up your horse, boss," said Shine. "With him thinking that we was jumping after him, coming out of the woods, and him with no gun except your empty one—how come you let him have that?"

"I dunno," said Calico.

He turned wearily back into the barn.

"You try and think, boss," urged Shine. "It don't seem like a natural thing for you to do."

"Nobody ever had my guns before," said Calico.

"You try to think why you'd leave him keep that gun

of yours," insisted Shine. "You gotta have a reason for that. You always gotta reason for everything."

"I think," said Calico, slowly, "that I couldn't take it off of a living man. He had to be dead, first. Like paying something first, and taking the gun afterwards. I think that was it."

"The mustang's gone," said Shine. "That was the most gun-loving horse I ever seen. It used to stand still and prick its ears like it wanted to eat the rabbit you was to shoot at. Yeah, or the man."

"Yes," sighed Calico. "Or the man."

"Where do we go now, boss?" asked Shine.

"We go to a place called Cannon Hill," said Calico.

"Hey! You gunna light a match on the top of Cannon Hill?" demanded the Negro.

"Yes," said Calico.

CHAPTER 20

Mary Layden

IT WAS a good deal earlier in the evening that Mary Layden sat in the dark of her room beside the window.

She never had known before how much one can see by the light of stars, even without a moon to help. The two hills were black and huge as mountains and seemed withdrawn to a distance, but the flash of the creek that ran between them was more intimate, more nearly. The northern was Cannon Hill and it was on Cannon Hill that she kept her eyes most of the time.

Behind her in the darkness Harry Layden kept on talking.

"You think you know something. You think you got something against The Streak. You haven't got anything. You haven't got anything real. He's as straight as they make 'em. This here Buck McGuire, and that long-drawn-out drink of water, that Bill Roan, what would they count for, anyway? They'd have to lie. They couldn't talk straight. All the claim they got to anybody noticing 'em was the fact that they knew The Streak. Now you tell me true—wasn't it something that the one of 'em said to you?"

She made no answer.

"Go on, Mary. You tell me, will you?" he insisted.

"If I said yes, what would you do, Harry?"

"I'd tear their hearts out, both of 'em, and throw 'em to the dogs," said Harry Layden. "Go on and tell me, Mary, will you?"

"Harry, I want to be alone, please," said the girl.

He got up. His chair squeaked as his big weight came off it. He came over and stood behind her in the dark. She felt his nearness like a warmth.

"Mary, how sorry I feel!" he said. "Don't go on sitting in the dark, like this. It breaks father all up. Mother takes it hard, but it's killing father. He's sick. He's terribly sick. I wish you'd try to come down and talk to them."

"If I had to talk to them, I think I'd cry," said Mary.

"That'd do you good," said Harry. "That's the best thing, to let it overflow and wash away. Everybody knows that."

"It wouldn't wash away. If I go down and cry, father will want to fight somebody. Talk to me about something else just a moment."

"Sure. I'll talk about anything you want. What I feel is that it was too good to last, anyway. I mean, it was too good to last when you think of what The Streak was like. There was never anybody else honest except The Streak. Guns and horses—who knew anything about guns and horses, outside of him?"

"I don't want to talk about Jim," she said.

"Well, go ahead, then."

"Who killed Philip B. Coles?"

"What in the world's the matter with you, Mary?"

"I was thinking about it."

"You don't mean you'd hitch a dirty crime like that to The Streak, do you?"

"Is there anybody in the world that knows the truth?" she asked.

"Nobody except Tenner."

"Does he know?"

"They say that he knows too much. Maybe not. Maybe it's only because he looks like such a pale rat that must have gnawed into the heart of a lot of secrets. But people say that he knows everything."

"He's a horrible creature," said the girl.

"He's a rat," repeated Harry.

"Will you let me be alone, now?" she asked.

"Yes . . . you can't come down and face the folks?"

"I can't very well do that. I'll do it in the morning," she said.

"It isn't one thing," he said. "It isn't that you're stopped caring about The Streak, is it?"

"No, it's not that," she answered.

"Good-by, old girl," said Harry.

He put his hand down and found her hair and patted it. He did not know how to caress. His fingers were tangling her hair. She wanted to cry out at him, but she kept silent. Women have to know how to be silent.

He went out of the room, and closed the door softly, reverently, as though there were a death inside it.

She kept on thinking that women need to know hardly anything, except always to be silent, silent. That will carry them through to the finish.

She could remember the half dozen great times when her mother had been silent, when her mother had swallowed knowledge with her eyes and never uttered a syllable of it with her lips.

After a while, Mary Layden stood up and went out of the house. She went down by the back stairs that entered the kitchen. Those stairs were narrow and the walls glimmered naked with brown paint. When people want to do things cheaply, why do they have to do them in the most ugly manner possible? Brown paint. And no rug to mute the footfall that made a clatter far through the house, when the cook came stumbling down in the morning.

The cool of the morning, a weary night behind, and school to face—that was the way Mary felt now; something like that, and really not worse. It would have been wrong if she had told herself that this misery was much greater. It was only that one knows school will pass; but this thing never would pass.

Suppose one considers the soul as a deep soil. All her soul was rooted through with one idea. The soil would have to be changed.

This present idea would have to go out of her before she could lose the pain that was in her.

She got the kitchen door open after a long time, she was so careful not to let it squeak. Then she went down the back porch steps to the ground, which was bare not with gravel but from the passing of horses, and the scratching of chickens. The pasture was close by. She went to the fence of it and called. One of the dark, lumpish figures on the ground got up, growing out of the black of the ground, as it were.

It got up so she could see the head and the long, slim neck. It came at a walk, then at a trot.

The yearling filly, Sally, pushed her head over the top of the fence. She reached for Mary's hand with a long, velvety upper lip. Her eyes shone. Prickling points of starlight were in them. And Mary pushed her hand down the incredible sleek of the neck.

The home had been such a place of utter peace before The Streak came into Jasper Valley. He had said: "Sally is the most beautiful thing in the world." He had looked straight into the eyes of Mary, smiling a little, nodding, and saying: "Sally is the most beautiful thing in the world!"

Remembering that, the pain grew colder and flowed deeper into the heart of Mary. It seemed to be rising, also up through her throat and as high as her lips, stifling her.

Dying, after all, would be something like this—darkness and breathlessness.

She turned. The filly snuffed hot breath down the back of her neck. She put up a hand and pressed the cheek of Sally against her own.

But that was no good. Horses don't understand caresses; only the one that help an itch, only the ones that scratch the skin. But to humans, there are times when the only sweet consolation in the world is the touch of a hand. Or the touch of an eye, even.

She started back towards the house. It was too big and black. It was like a monument, and the tall trees that ran

down the driveway were cemetery trees, solemn and tall
and still.

She went into the barn, saddled a horse, and rode on to
the town.

CHAPTER 21

Baldwin Disappears

THE night was warm. The gelding began to sweat. It
hadn't been trained for the work of steady riding, and
its flesh was all grass flesh, soft, easily melted. The smell
of the sweat was a good thing though, because it was
familiar.

When The Streak came into the house, fresh from riding, there often was a smell of horse sweat about him. If
you came close to him, there was a sort of barn-savor
about him. That never had struck her before, but it was
true. It was rather disgusting, perhaps, but not disgusting
to Mary.

She thought: If a woman is easily disgusted, she'll never
get on through the world. Take husbands, for instance.
They don't stay the same all through life. Not by a very
great deal. Boys fall in love most easily in the spring. For
that matter, there is a gay, warm, bright time in their
early lives when men are able to love more quickly and
strongly. But afterwards, there isn't so much of that. The
women have children and the men have work and only
the kind God can keep the love flowing between them.

But a woman can be patient. If a brutal word or a
savage look can disgust her, the love will die out. Love
between a man and a woman needs tending like a garden.
The best soil in the world will turn to desert or jungle,
unless it's tended. And a queer sense of strength came
into the heart and the hands of Mary, because she felt
that she, at least, would know how to tend it and make
it grow—a garden that time could only render more beautiful.

The lights of familiar houses shone through the night.

The one that was high enough and thin enough to be a star was from the Townsend place on the hill. She could name all the others. Jasper was not a very big place but when one could name all the lights in it, it meant something. Some people can name all the stars, and they are the ones who love to watch the sky by night.

If only her mother or father did not go up to her room and find her gone! But this was a heavenly comfort, to ride through the streets of Jasper, by night. Even the alkaline, sharp odor of the dust was pleasant to her. All things familiar are a delight to the sorrowing, perhaps.

But if she looked left, if she looked right, the lights turned into faces that she knew, and every face was full of smiling kindness. How many people there were who would give her, with both their hands, from the heart, all the happiness they could. Enough happiness, one would think, to be garnered up and kept all one's life. But that was not the way it could happen. Hands and hearts cannot give you happiness.

It is something that slides in through the eyes, as music flows through the ears. One evening the skies open and you can ride right straight on into the brightness of the heavens; and all the other evenings only serve to make you feel the black rim of the earth and the narrow of it, and the long, long, long darkness.

Off there on the left was the house of Philip B. Coles. When she saw the light glimmering down through the trees, she was startled and halted her horse. Why should there be a light in that house?

And then she remembered Tenner. Of course, Tenner was up there. Anybody else would be afraid to live alone in such an empty, great house with a whisper and the chill of death still adrift in its shadows. But Tenner was different. Tenner was the sort of a fellow who would not be startled by ghosts. He, rather, would be a companion of them.

Suppose she rode up to that house, now, and knocked at the front door, and listened to the echo of the knock go climbing the stairs and dimly down the halls; suppose she heard a stealthy step coming to answer her at the door. Suppose that the door opened, slowly, and there against the black of the interior she were to see the long,

pale face of Tenner; suppose, even, that she said: "Mr.
Tenner, I think you know. Tell me who murdered Mr.
Philip B. Coles. I'll never speak of what you tell me. But
my soul is dying. There's no breath or air left for me
to breathe. Because I don't know the truth. Will you tell
it to me?"

She closed her eyes. A chill was working up her spine.
The breath actually was leaving her, at the thought of
such an encounter.

Still with her eyes closed, she allowed the horse to move
on. And that was good, because when she looked out
again, they would be past the house of Coles.

But now the horse lurched a little over a hollow in the
way and then its feet began to grind in gravel.

She opened her eyes then, amazed, and found herself
entering the driveway of the Coles place, with the tall,
black trees going up on either side and shutting out the
stars.

It was horrible miracle that the gelding should have
turned in at this place, in keeping with her thoughts—but
then she remembered that the gelding was one of those
that will always take any left hand turning, unless it is
checked. You'd think that some horses had no brains at
all, the way they close their eyes and let silly instincts
befool them.

And yet she could not rein the gelding back and turn
him around. She was atremble with fear, and yet it seemed
to Mary that, from the moment she left her room, something like fate had been drawing her forward, step by
step, until she found herself going up the driveway of the
Coles place. It was like entering a dream.

Suppose she went to the house—suppose even that she
spoke to Tenner—what could she say, really?

And still in that cold of nightmare, the gelding carried
her on up the driveway and to the opening in the trees
in front of the house, where dead Mrs. Coles used to
maintain her charming garden. Now it was all black brush
that looked up at her in mound after mound. The face of
the house was a tall, empty shadow, with guilty knowledge
behind it.

He had been shot right between the eyes. Only a cool,
confident man would dream of selecting such a spot as his

target. Most murderers would try for the heart. Afterwards they might finish off the victim with a shot through the head. But a cool, confident man who could not make a mistake with his guns—a man like The Streak, would shoot for the head. One bullet, just between the eyes. And then he would watch the body slide sideways out of the chair, and slump onto the floor. That would be the thing. The Streak standing there, calmly watchful, indifferent. He needed money. He would make up his mind that the life of the moneylender was no good to anyone, really. He had that cold, clear way of dealing with events, everyone said. Most of the time he was a little dreamy. Rather like a child, in some respects. But when it came to action—ah, then he suddenly was the clear steel that took the finest edge!

There was no light in the front of the house. She pulled the gelding over to the driveway that went past the side of the house towards the stable. There, before her, she saw the glimmering of a light. The gelding walked on. The way beneath was soft with grass that the last rains had made green. The falling of the hoofs made only a whisper in the grass. It seemed as though the horse were stalking.

So she came to the open window and the light streamed out into her face.

The window, for one on the first floor, was quite high, but from her elevation in the saddle, she could look easily over the sill and see the ranged books of a library. It was one of those old family libraries, all the editions being of about 1885. Something had come over the world at about that time, it seemed to Mary Layden, and all the houses in Jasper Valley had sets of Walter Scott and Charles Dickens and Thackeray, and all the great old names. She knew the dingy look of them.

She looked over these books with a sigh, and then she saw a hand go up to the topmost shelf and take down a book.

It shocked Mary Layden, though it was a simple enough thing to see.

Tenner had come in to get something for reading himself to sleep, that night. That was it.

She listened. She could hear the rustling and the flickering noise of pages being rapidly turned.

Then she saw the book placed back on the shelf, and the arm and hand rose to take down another book. It was rather odd that Tenner, slender as he was, should have such a brown, powerful hand and wrist.

She rose in her stirrups. Her view of the room was instantly doubled and redoubled, and she saw that the man in the room was no less than the very greatest man in Jasper Valley. It was, in fact, Perry T. Baldwin himself!

She was so astonished, so delighted, that she remained, standing in the stirrups, staring.

All the ghostly fear had in an instant vanished away from her. For where Perry T. Baldwin was, there was nothing to be feared. The whole strong force of the law seemed to be represented in the resolute, strong square of his shoulders. Wisdom, truth, vision, justice resided in that big head of his.

The girl began to smile a little. She thought of calling out to him, but it would seem a very strange thing, indeed, if she were to call out through a window, as though she came spying about the Coles house in the middle of the night—or almost the middle, as it seemed to her.

He went on with his work of taking down volume after volume. First he shook the book. Then holding it by the back, he flicked the pages as though waiting for something to fall to the floor. And after that, not content with this summary procedure, he held the book in a normal position and flicked over the leaves rapidly.

He was searching for something. It was very odd that even a man as rich as Philip B. Coles should have in his house something of real importance to a person like Perry Baldwin.

She reined her horse around and rode back to the front of the house. There she paused again. There was a pleasant excitement in her mind. She wanted, very much, to see and speak with Perry T. Baldwin. If she could only think for a moment, she would find a theme. It hardly mattered what. Perry Baldwin was all ready to speak with anyone. That was one of his values—his intense democracy.

She dismounted and threw the reins of the horse. She

was going up the steps of the front veranda, then. And
at last she was dropping the battered knocker against the
front door. The echo ran back dimly through the house,
just as she had expected. But she felt not the slightest
fear.

It was true that Perry Baldwin had taken a very strong
stand, indeed, in the hunt he organized against The Streak,
but only a very silly woman indeed would attribute that
to anything other than his love of the law and his hatred
of criminals. And his presence in this house was more
reassuring to her than the light and the warmth of the
noonday sun would have been. By far more!

As she had expected, too, a faintly heard footfall came
towards the door, and as she had expected, it was slowly
pulled open.

Only a little open, and she saw the ghostly pallor, the
ghostly dimness of the face of Tenner.

The door pulled suddenly wide open, as he made her
out by the faint light that streamed over his shoulder
from the interior of the hall.

She could see, now, his strange grinning look.

"Good evening, Mr. Tenner," she said. "I was told
that Mr. Baldwin could be found here."

Tenner held onto the knob of the door with one hand
and rested the other agianst the jamb. He kept grinning
and nodding his head.

He said: "Oh, they told you that Perry T. Baldwin was
here, did they? Who is they, Miss Layden? I wonder
who 'they' may be?"

She had no answer for that. But it was not necessary
to answer all the strange remarks that might be made by
a queer fellow like Tenner.

"I'd like to see him," she said.

"You'd like to see him— She would like to see Perry
T. Baldwin," and laughed a little, slowly running his eyes
over her.

"Ah, but he isn't here?" she asked, growing a trifle
nervous.

"Why, I think he is," said Tenner. "Yes, I'm sure he
is. Just step this way, Miss Layden. Just step this way."

He went on before her, nodding his head a little to
himself, amused so that his shoulders quivered. And she

followed on through the half dismantled hallway, noticing how it had begun to collect dust, so that the footprints which had crossed it before her showed clearly enough. She felt a touch of indignation that Tenner had allowed the place to run down so fast after the death of Philip B. Coles. Of course, all servants are that way. If you want things done properly, do them with your own hands, said the old family maxim.

At a door just down the hall—it must have been the door to the library, she was sure—Tenner paused.

"Something important, ain't it?" he asked. "Lot of important things have been talked about in this library, here. A lot of 'em!"

He turned again and threw the door open. There was only blank darkness inside. She stared at it with eyes that would not believe.

Tenner was peering into the gloom, also.

"Why, he must of left," said Tenner. "He was in here, sure enough. Finishing off some sort of business between him and Philip B. Coles. But he must of took it into his head to leave, quick. He must of gone out the side or back door."

He hung onto the knob of the door and turned back to her, slowly closing the door behind him.

"What you wanted to see Perry T. Baldwin about? I couldn't do you no good, could I?" asked Tenner.

His lip twitched back into the start of a laugh that stopped, and froze in place. And all at once the life went out of her. She felt the breath go.

"I've got to—I've got to get home," she said.

"Ah, you've got to go home, have you?" said Tenner.

He came right up to her. And she could not move.

It *was* a nightmare into which the gelding had carried her. This was the frightful, ice cold heart of it. She could not run. Her legs were stopped with a paralysis. And the creature who was not a man was there walking towards her, calmly, assured that she could not flee. He came and took her by the arm.

"It's this way, if you want to get out," said Tenner.

She turned and went with him. She saw each of the dusty footprints in the hallways clearly. She saw the bulk of the great closed front door, strong enough to have secured the safety of a fortress. And then that door was opened by Tenner.

He still kept his small, bony hand gripping her arm hard enough to bruise it.

"Sorry you couldn't find Perry T. Baldwin," he said. "Sorry that *they* told you he was here, and that then you couldn't find him. Sorry about that. Maybe you'll find him next time—if you look hard enough. There's a lot to be said for good, hard looking. Good night, Miss Layden. Good night."

He began to laugh and could not stop. He kept on laughing, and through the laughter his bright little eyes gleamed at her, followed her, rushed up behind her when her back was turned to go down the front steps of the house.

She was in the saddle, and could not tell how she got there. And then panic made her drive her horse down the driveway at full speed, so fast that it stumbled as it struck the slippery dust and veered into the lengthwise of the street.

CHAPTER 22

Mary Layden, Nurse

SHE traveled out towards her home through the lights of Jasper Valley. She did not at all feel as though she were going home. She felt, rather, as though there were no possible destination. There was no end of the road for her.

It was not late. It was early in the night and the lights shone from every house even from the shack of that old miser, Ralph Waters. And she among those lights traveled darkly, like a cloud among the stars, unvisited, uncomforted.

She wanted to put things together. There was something about Perry T. Baldwin searching the books in the library of Philip Coles's house. There was something about that which was important. It was something she could figure out, almost, if only the horse would stop walking. And then she felt assured that, walking or stopped still under the stars, she never would be able to fathom the thing. It needed a cleverer brain than hers. And yet it *was* important. Why should Perry T. Baldwin be there in the dark of the night and slip away from the house secretly, when a girl he had known all her life came to the place to see him? Or had Baldwin known? Had he simply finished whatever he had come for and so gone away? No, that was not the attitude of Tenner. Tenner had been surprised.

Mary Layden turned her horse into the driveway to her house, but she halted the gelding willingly enough when she heard the pattering of the hoofs of another horse come down the main highway towards her. She had a vague hope that it might be someone she knew, and any pause for conversation would have been welcome, rather than to go back to the darkness of the great, black house, where the sad, watchful eyes of her family had to be met—had to be met either this night or tomorrow morning.

She saw the coming rider, the wind of the gallop furling the brim of his sombrero. Even by the starlight she could see that. And now he swung his long-striding horse suddenly to the side, and into the very driveway where she was waiting.

"Jim!" she cried out. The rider jerked his horse violently aside, and cried out. Then he pulled Rocket over to her. "Mary?" he said. "Mary? Out here? Mary?" He kept repeating that.

"I had to go into town," she said.

"Why did you have to go into town?" asked Blondy.

"I had to go," she said. "I thought you'd be away over the hills and out of Jasper Valley forever, Jim."

"I thought so, too," he said. "But I couldn't go."

"Why couldn't you go, Jim?"

"I don't know. I couldn't go . . . I'll take you back up to the house, if you don't mind riding beside me. I mean, if it doesn't make you feel dirty and mean to have me beside you."

"Oh, Jim!"

"I know," said Blondy. "It isn't that you hate me, It's

only that it sort of sickens you to think about me. Because you think that I killed him—the old man, I mean—Philip B. Coles. You think I did that, don't you?"

She looked up, and all the stars lifted in the sky and burned across her mind.

"Yes, I think that," she said.

"But you don't mind me riding up to the house with you?"

"Oh, Jim! Oh, Jim! Of course I don't mind. But you ought not to be here in Jasper Valley."

"I had to stay. I couldn't go," he said.

"Why couldn't you go?"

"I tried to go. But I couldn't. I kept thinking."

"About—about *him?*"

"I kept thinking about you . . . You know, Mary, you'd think that pride would keep a man from even thinking about a girl that doesn't believe in him any more. But pride doesn't stop me. I keep thinking about you. I tell you, there's a kind of star-dust in the air, and a sweetness, the minute I even think about you. I can pick out the thought of the Layden house from the whole world and thinking of it is pain and happiness all at one time. D'you know what I mean? Pain and happiness together . . . What's the matter, Mary?"

"Nothing," she said.

"I've sickened you. I've made you cry again," said Blondy.

"I'm not crying," said Mary Layden. "I'm just—I don't know what's happening to me."

"That means you still like me a good deal," said Blondy. "So it's still hard for you, a little. I mean, it's hard for you to tear up the idea of me by the roots and throw it away forever. Isn't that true?"

"Yes, that's true," she said. "I don't want to throw away the idea of you forever. I'll never forget you, Jim. I only . . ."

"Don't talk about me," he said. "Let's talk about something else."

"Yes, Jim," she said.

"About why you went down town. What you did and who you saw. Tell me about that, Mary."

"I don't want to talk about that."

"What *do* you want to say?"

"I want to say how I'm still loving you, Jimmy."

"Do you?" said Blondy. "Ah, I know. And that's always the way. You can't believe. It doesn't seem possible that I'm a rat. And yet you know that I am. You feel sure of it. You feel sure, as though you saw me standing there in the room and crashing the bullet through the head of Coles. Isn't that the way you feel?"

"Yes," she said.

"Don't cry any more, Mary."

"I'm not going to," she said. "But I feel a little sick, Jim."

"So do I," he said. "Tell me about things. How's your mother and father?"

"They're all right. I mean, they're not all right. Father's taking it terribly hard; and so is mother. They just look at me as though I'd done some terrible thing, sending you away. I think Harry almost hates me."

"Good old Harry. . . . Tell me where you've been, Mary."

"I had to get out of the house. I rode down town and found myself at the Coles house. It's too queer to put into words. I can't explain just how I happened to get there. As though I were drawn there. And then I went down the old driveway beside the house and looked through the lighted window and saw who do you think?"

"I can't guess. That odd fellow Tenner, perhaps?"

"A hand that took down book after book very carefully. I stood up in the stirrups and I could see him to the waist, and it was Perry T. Baldwin!"

"Baldwin? There in the Coles house? Searching?"

"It does seem strange, doesn't it?"

"Yes. It does. I don't know why it should, particularly. He and Coles were friends. There may have been something about business that Baldwin wanted to find."

"But to go searching there at night!"

"Why, Baldwin is pretty busy . . . When I came down the valley I could hear the donkey engine and the clicking of the hammers over there at the place where they're building the station . . . I mean, Baldwin is pretty busy, and he might have been working tonight and remembered all at once something that he had left at the Coles house."

"I suppose that's it. Still, it seemed strange."

"Yes, it does seem a little strange . . . Here's the house. Good-by, Mary. You mind asking Harry to step out and speak to me?"

"I can't. Harry went down town."

"Did he? Well, it's all right, then."

He swung down from the saddle and held out his hand.

"Good-by, Mary," he said. "I'll take the horse and put him up for you. You go on into the house."

"I wish you'd kiss me, Jim," she said.

"I can't," said Blondy. "I mean, my face is—well, it's too dirty."

"What have you been doing? Blondy, what *is* the matter! There's something sticky on your shirt. Will you step over here into the light from the window?"

He said: "No, it's all right. I've got to get along."

But still he yielded to her touch. She seemed strong enough to draw him here and there as she pleased; and so she drew him into the dim light from the window . . . and she saw . . .

"Jim!" she whispered, and gripped him by both arms.

"I didn't mean you to see," said Blondy. "It's nothing . . ."

"Jim, have they killed you? Are you dying? Jim, are you dying?"

"I'm hardly scratched. I'm all right. It was only a tap over the head. I've got to get along . . ."

"You come with me. You come into the house."

"I can't let your father and mother see all this."

"They won't see. There's warm water in the kitchen. I'll wash your head clean and put on a bandage. Jim, are you in terrible pain?"

"I don't think so," said Blondy.

"Come inside. Don't try to pull away from me. I'll scream and rouse up everybody if you won't come. Jim, please come along with me."

He went, compelled by her hands, and they crossed the back porch and opened the kitchen door. Her hands fumbled on a shelf. Matches rattled in a box. She struck a light and from the shading cup of her hands she threw one flash of the light upon him. He could see her lips part and her eyes shine blank and white. Then she lifted the chimney of a lamp and touched the flame to the circular burner.

The flame ran around the wick. The fire blazed up until she pushed the chimney down. Then the flame steadied, died, burning small and bright. There was no shade on the lamp. It cast a glare on everything in the kitchen because the walls were so white. The stove had been polished that evening; the taint of the burned polish remained in the air; a kettle still steamed slightly on the front of the stove.

She went and got the kettle,, keeping her eyes still askance on Blondy. She poured some water into a basin of granite ware and tempered it with water from the tap and felt the heat of the mixture with her hands.

"Put your head over the sink—over the basin, Jim," she said.

He rested his elbows on the edge of the sink and she began to wash his head. Wherever her fingers touched him, he felt their trembling.

She said: "Am I hurting you terribly? Is it terrible, Jim?"

"No," he said. "It's not terrible. It's all right."

"The scalp—it's all loose . . . it has to be sewed up . . . I've got to get you to a doctor, Jim."

"You tie a towel around it, and it'll be all right," said Blondy. "It doesn't hurt. It seems as though you've washed all the pain away. If I were dying, Mary, I think your hands would catch back the life and give it to me again. I never knew of hands like yours, Mary."

The basin ran all full of bloody water, and his head was lightened, eased.

She made him sit down in a chair and then out of a long runner towel she made a bandage that ran around and around his head.

"It's only good enough to last until you see the doctor," she said. "Dr. Jeffers is the man for you to see. He's the one who loves you, Jim. You go straight to him, will you?"

He stood up. "Ah!" cried Mary. "Jim! Look!"

She started around towards him, still pointing out the kitchen window, and as he stared through the open win-

dow he saw on the top of Cannon Hill the gleam of a
small light, a light almost too small to be seen, that
penciled its dim strokes up and down, up and down, and
then went out.

CHAPTER 23

Calico's Treachery

BLONDY gripped the edge of the sink. Some of his weight
came on his arms and they shuddered under the burden
as he stared at the place where the light had been.

"Calico" he whispered. "He found your letter on me.
He's trying to call you—Calico—"

His voice went out. Then something about her silence
made him glance at her, and he saw her transfixed,
staring at the trembling terror in his body, and the cold
frost of fear in his face. He swallowed.

"Calico! It's Calico Charlie!" he whispered.

"Are you afraid?" said the girl in a strained, small
voice.

He could not answer. All the fear in the world was in
him, and she was standing there to see it. She felt that he
was a murderer. Now she could see that he was a coward,
too. He lifted his hand, without thinking, to the bandage
that went around his head, and he saw a swimming sick-
ness in her eyes. She was white around the mouth, with
nausea. She would understand.

Calico Charlie had beaten the vaunted courage out of
him and turned him into a cur.

He wanted to say a great many things. But he closed
his eyes. There were explanations of everything, but they
never would be believed. He was, to her, The Streak,
and therefore his career was as true and clear as the
light of the moon in the heavens. She believed in the
brillant career of The Streak as she believed in her God;
and if that career had turned the dark corner as far as
murder, what was murder compared with shameful terror?

"Well, good-by," said Blondy.

He held out his hand towards her, but all she could see was the dying soul in his eyes. She did not make a gesture to take his hand.

He backed up and found the door. He went out into the darkness, closing the door behind him, and she did not move to stop him; she did not speak a word.

He got to his horse. Now, as he looked back over things, he could see a clear explanation of everything. His career in Jasper Valley had been a great absurd romance. In Jasper Valley he had done nothing—and yet every man in the valley except Calico Charlie and Shine would swear that he was a giant killer. He had grown to so great a fame that, at last, his reputation was clinging to him like his skin. He could not throw it away without worse than dying.

He had died just now in the mind of Mary Layden. He had turned from a hero into a dreadful creature of sham and shame. And that was worse than being beaten over the head; that was worse than being brained by a blow; worse than having bullets tear through the flesh to the heart.

He got into the saddle. The horse started moving. It went into a trot . . . And Calico Charlie was off there on Cannon Hill waiting, lighting his damned matches, waiting. Rocket began to gallop. Suddenly big Blondy was shouting aloud.

He drove Rocket to the dizzy full of his speed all the way across the hollow, past the dim starlit gleam of the creek, and up the zigzag slope of Cannon Hill to the crest. There were woods scattered all the way to the top, scraggly, poor stuff. But the top of Cannon Hill was bare and open. People said that it commanded one of the finest of all the views of Jasper Valley. And it looked down, for Blondy, on the house of the Laydens, with one or two lights shining from it.

He shouted. "Calico! Calico Charlie! You hear me? It's The Streak—you dirty dog—you damned dirty rat— It's The Streak calling to you. You hear me? Come here and get your windup! Come on and talk turkey with me!"

His breath went out of him. He waited, panting. The smell of the sweat of the horse rose to his nostrils. Some-

thing creaked behind him. He jerked around in the saddle.
For a weapon, he had the long unloaded Colt that belonged to Calico, and had belonged to a greater man before him.

But there was nothing coming up behind him. It was
only a creaking of the saddle leather as big Rocket stirred
uneasily, anxious for some more hard galloping.

The woods stood black around him, fencing him in.
It was as good a place as any to die in. The buzzards
would find a body quickly up here. It would be torn to
rags and tatters before human eyes ever found him. But
that was better than dying alive in the eyes of Mary
Layden.

"Calico!" he shouted. "Hey, Calico! It's The Streak.
Cal-i-co!" He yelled the name with all his power, but
there was no answer.

Why should he expect one, for that matter? Calico was
not the fool to announce his deadly comings and goings. If
a fool asked to be murdered, Calico would come with
expedition and shoot the fool through the back, with
precision. Calico was certainly not aiming a gun at The
Streak from the sheltered safe edge of the woods. Even
by starlight, Calico could not miss at a distance like this.

Fear went by the heart of Blondy like an arrow, but
the wind of it did not blow his soul cold.

And he was amazed. It was as though, having died in
spirit down there in the Layden kitchen, in the wide eyes
of Mary Layden, he now had nothing left inside him that
could fear death. His body was nothing. Why, the smash
of a bullet going through his heart would be no more
pain than the crash of the gunbutt against his head that
evening, or the toe of Calico's boot cracking against his
chin.

"Calico! Calico! You dirty dog, are you afraid?" he
yelled.

Because Calico had to be there in hearing distance,
surely. Calico who had sneaked up there like a foul thief
and tried to lure a girl out to him—Calico must be somewhere, waiting for her coming.

"Calico! Calico!" shouted Blondy.

And then he knew, suddenly, that Calico was not coming.

Perhaps on the way down from the summit, Calico would be lurking and waiting for a surer, safer shot.

That was what would happen. So he rode back down the trail with his eyes keenly stabbing into the darkness and the long, unloaded gun of Calico Charlie at a balance, resting on top of the pommel of the saddle.

Rocket snorted and sidestepped. It was not from a living shadow that stirred in the woods, but from the pale face of a glassy boulder.

And that was all. All the way to the bottom of Cannon Hill, that was all that happened.

Perhaps Calico Charlie did not like fighting in the dark of the night, where some of his skill with guns would be wasted? No, the saying was that the tiger in Calico Charlie preferred the night to the open day.

Back onto the highway rode big Blondy, shaking his head. And when he shook his head, he felt a little pain, and it seemed to him that the fingers of Mary Layden, losing their gentleness, had gripped him hard and were torturing his flesh.

The highway led over a small rise of the ground. Off to the side, he could hear the clinking hammers and the coughing donkey engine from the estate of Perry T. Baldwin. where the work went on by day and by night.

"Perry T. Baldwin, you be damned," said The Streak.

He waved his hands at the lights of Jasper. They all could be damned. He wanted this thing over with.

That was why he rode straight into Jasper. The lights from the houses went out over the street and paved the dust with soft yellow, gold. It was not very late. It was early, in fact. Nobody was in bed. And those who were up would hear guns before the morning, if he had his way.

He stopped in front of the shop of Jeff Wilkes, who sold fishing tackle and guns and cutlery, and all that sort of thing.

Wilkes was an old gray silent fellow with a face like a hatchet and harder than the hatchet's steel. He lived in a pair of rooms over his shop.

"Hey, Wilkes! Hello! Wilkes!" shouted The Streak.

And after his big shout died down into an echo, he heard the dry, calm voice of Wilkes speak out of the dark of a window above him: "Hello, Streak, what you want?"

"Come down and open your shop," said The Streak. "I want some ammunition, brother, and I want it now."

"I'll come down," said Wilkes, and there was the noise of his chair pushing back. The chair made a stuttering brief thunder on the board of the floor. Then the step of Wilkes came with deliberation down the stairs at the side of the shop.

CHAPTER 24

No Fear of Calico

WHILE that footfall went down the stairs, big Blondy dismounted and began to rub the wet jowl of his horse and stare at the sky. That night he was to die; and a man about to die ought to look around him and take in the beauty of the world in deeper draughts than he ever has done before. No wind should blow except winds of music.

The stars should burn lower in heaven with beauty. But they were not burning any lower for Blondy. He could bend back his head and take in the bright speckling swarm in the sky, but his mind went back to another picture—a gun gripped in the little claws of Calico Charlie, the muzzle of it jerking up in rapid vibrations as the shots were poured forth; and his own body torn and battered by those shots tearing through the flesh, thudding home like heavy fists, smashing the bones. That was the picture he kept seeing blown across the stars.

The thing would not last long. That was the redeeming part of it. Calico Charlie's guns finished their business with speed.

Afterwards, someone would bring the news to Mary Layden, and if they told her that he had died, they also would have to say that he had sought out Calico Charlie of his own volition; and if he showed her, that night, his fear of Calico, she would understand in the end that he had dreaded shame more than dying.

Thinking of this, it seemed to him that the world about him was dim and trivial.

The footfall of Wilkes had passed from the inside stairs to the floor of the shop. Now a lamp was lighted. The illumination struck through the window into his face. He saw the lank form of Wilkes cross to the door, which was opened.

"Come on in, Streak," said Wilkes.

He stood back with a strange amount of ceremony and yet of mockery in his manner and in his face. Blondy felt that he was being bowed to from in front and laughed at behind his back. He went over to a glass counter with a case of guns exposed beneath. They were all shotguns. The steel was blue-black. It had a rich shimmer. The fine steel was no thicker than heavy paper. If he had one of those double-barreled beauties loaded with buckshot, he would have a better chance against Calico Charlie, But that wouldn't be in the tradition of The Streak. The user of a shotgun is a brutal fellow who goes out to kill his rabbit or his squirrel—or his man! The weapon of Western chivaly is the revolver. Rules of the game go along with it. Every fellow must have a chance to fill his hand. You come in through the front door and say: "Smith, I'm going to be waiting at the corner of Second and Main Streets this afternoon at three o'clock. I hope that you'll be able to meet me there."

Then you say good-by and that afternoon you take your stand at the street corner. And presently a voice calls out your name. You whirl, drawing your gun.

That's the sort of technique. You have to follow that procedure, or else it's apt to be called murder. Western juries are very lenient, in certain parts of the country, but every now and then they fail to endorse the classic plea of "self-defense."

And then Blondy wondered if, after all, things ever had happened that way. Was it not all a matter of tradition, legend, and many foolish stories written into the books? When men fought with fists or guns, was there anything knightly about it, or wasn't it usually a matter of a brawl, a savage flurry of words, voices suddenly cursing, and then: "Take this, damn you!"

Well, it didn't much matter what actually happened all

over the world. The truth was that he was in the grip of a legend about himself. And since the world expected The Streak to act as the perfect knight, above fear and reproach, he, Blondy, had at last to lay down his life for the sake of the high reputation of a name.

"Just the old forty-five calibre stuff, Wilkes," he had heard his lips say. "Just enough to load the old gun once."

He pulled out the huge Colt of Calico Charlie.

"Just six cartridges?" asked Wilkes.

"No, just five," said Blondy.

"You keep one chamber empty for luck, Streak? asked Wilkes.

"You take a hair-trigged affair like this," said Blondy, "and you have to be careful; you can't let the hammer rest on a full chamber. See?"

He flicked the hammer of the gun lightly with his thumb. It rose and clicked back rapidly.

"I see," said Wilkes. "How long it take you, Streak, to learn to fan a gun like that?"

Blondy looked up towards the ceiling. He laughed a little. To stand at a counter, holding the gun with one hand and flicking the hammer of it with the thumb of the other hand—that was simple, of course. But to be able to stand up and shoot for a mark, flicking the hammer of the gun with the thumb of the hand that held it—had any of even the most famous old gunmasters been able to accomplish the thing? Or was it chiefly talk, rumor, legend again—always legend. Fairy stories grow as tall and as blue as the mountains, near any country's frontier.

"You laugh, eh?" said Wilkes. "But I suppose you must have taken a good ten years to learn the trick of it. To stand off and stream the bullets like it was an automatic firing."

Yes, that was the way legend grew. Blondy felt himself in the breath-taking presence of its birth at that moment. Wilkes would say, out of his own mind, that The Streak had spent ten years mastering the complicated art of fanning a revolver. Wilkes would say that The Streak with his own lips had told him so. Before morning Wilkes would be assured in his own mind that the thing had been spoken so.

And now, to complete the legend Blondy knew that he must not stand before Calico Charlie in the orthodox fashion, with his forefinger on the trigger, trying to plant a lucky shot that might end the battle in his favor. That chance would not be much better, against the skill of Calico Charlie in murder, than was the chance of the condemned man who was given the pitiful little stylus with which to face the charge of the lion in the arena. But even that chance Blondy must cast away because the pitiless legend of The Streak demanded that he should fan the hammer of his revolver, streaming out the shots.

"And yet you know what I think?" said Wilkes. "I wonder why you wouldn't take an automatic, if you want to fire fast. Just give the trigger one good squeeze, and there's an end of the thing. Every bullet is out of that gun in less'n a second. Why wouldn't you use an automatic?"

And again Blondy laughed a little, for he was thinking that the reason he had not carried an automatic was that he never had thought of buying one. Besides, that wouldn't be a nice clean killing, for using an automatic would be as bad, almost, as fighting a duel with a shotgun. The Streak couldn't use an automatic.

He said: "I wouldn't use an automatic, Wilkes."

"I know," said Wilkes. "They jam. That's what they do. They jam. A fellow like you, Streak—how you feel when you see the other fellow drop? I always wanted to ask that of somebody like you. How you feel when the other fellow turns into old rags and just slumps down on the ground or slings out of the saddle with his going full speed? How you feel about it?"

"Oh, I don't know," said Blondy.

"You don't know! You don't care! It's just the old, old story, eh?" said Wilkes.

He rubbed his lean chops and stared curiously into the face of Blondy. "I hope you don't make no mistake, sometime," he said. "I hope they don't have the hanging of you to do, sometime. What I mean, we all like you fine. You know that. But suppose you got careless, sometime, is what I mean. I mean, not caring much one way or the other, a fellow might get careless, mightn't he?"

"I suppose so," said Blondy.

He was tempted to say something else. All his nerves jumped with the high voltage of an electric shock. It would be burning his bridges behind him; it would be publishing his determination to the world; it would be closing the door against all retreat. And yet he said it.

"Are Calico Charlie and Shine in town, Wilkes?"

"I dunno. They might be down at Pete Reilly's place, I suppose."

"I'll go down there and see," said Blondy.

"You going down there? Down to Pete Reilly's? Streak, listen to me. They don't like you very well down at Pete Reilly's. You don't have no friends down there at Pete's. They're all the ones that are kind of down on you."

"I know," answered Blondy. "But I want to find Calico and Shine before the night's ended. Well, so long, Wilkes."

He tossed money onto the counter. A dollar would pay for five cartridges several times over. But The Streak had to pay in this manner. He had to be a man above money. A man who threw money away as though it were dirt.

Now he stood in the open air again beside his horse. Rocket pushed out an inquiring head and pricked his ears. The star points were shining in the big eyes of the gelding.

He took the fine silk of one of those ears and stripped it softly through his fingers. Even Rocket had been cheated. Chance and the scourge of thirst had broken the spirit of the wild horse, and by the cheat he had been induced to love one master. A chance like that, blended with so many other chances, seemed more than circumstance. It seemed, indeed, like an act of Fate.

The idea came swiftly, coldly rushing like night over the soul of Blondy. Perhaps, after all, there is a divinity thinner than the blue of the sky, stronger than the hard hand of iron, and bent on shaping the ways which men must follow. In that case, to what end was he being brought? At any rate, there is no resisting the high decrees.

All the burden, it seemed to Blondy, of decisions of all kinds was removed from him. He had only to go straight forward along the new path; and since death and

Calico Charlie waited for him along the way, there was no avoiding that destiny.

Then he thought of Mary Layden; and his heart sank, like a stone weltering down through a dark well.

CHAPTER 25

The Streak's Triumph

JIMMY, at this time, was supposed to be in bed. In fact he had kissed his parents good night, reached his room, taken off his shoes, dropped them with heavy clumping sounds on the floor, and then lying down on the bed he had caused the springs to creak loudly and had made certain sighing and groaning sounds.

Afterwards he tied his shoes around his neck and stole out through the window of his room and so on to the slant roof of the kitchen. Happy and silent and fierce as a cat that has dozed all day in the warm corners of the house, he wakened in the night. Everything was different. The trees were twice as tall as the sun ever saw them and they assumed new shapes, threatening, mysterious.

But there was no fear in Jimmy because he carried with him a magic weapon. It was the big Colt which once, the tradition said, had been the gun of Wild Bill and since that time had become the gun of Calico Charlie; but the greatest benediction of all was that it had been touched by the hands of The Streak.

To remain another moment in the house with such a treasure was absurd. Jimmy wanted to go out into the country of the night where robbers walk abroad and all the tigerish humans are prowling. Among them he could pass with an enchanted safety. If the gun was empty that did not matter; it was still Excalibur.

So he slipped down the drain pipe from the eaves and got out onto Main Street. He had no exact plan, but he could go lurking from tree to tree, marking down left and right the lights of the houses which afterwards he would return with his robber band and plunder.

He was almost in the center of town when a rider jogged down the street. Jimmy slid behind a tree, so that the shadow of its trunk soaked up all token of his slender body. Around the edge of the big tree he peered forth and saw the rider passing through a shaft of lamplight that streamed out of the house of Widow Jenkins. The rider was obscured by night, but the sight of the horse made Jimmy jump. A yell ran up into his throat and lodged there, his lips opened and froze in place. He did not utter a sound, but he felt as though he had been screaming.

For the horse was Rocket and that meant that the rider was The Streak!

The Streak in person in the town of Jasper, where a hundred men were hungry for the blood money. The Streak in the Main Street of Jasper, riding along unconcerned!

Jimmy crossed the road, running low and hard, the weight of the long-barreled Colt jouncing up and down, promising to tear its way out of his clothes. He clasped the Colt to his breast with one hand and still made famous speed until he was only a little distance behind the jogging horse.

That was the miracle of it. A sweeping race through town and a couple of pistol shots left echoing behind, would have been understandable, but why this calm jogging?

Rocket stopped in the most incredible place in the world. He paused in front of the saloon of Pete Reilly!

And now—Jimmy, on one knee behind a tree, panting heavily, strangling to keep that panting from being heard, saw the rider dismount. No light from the windows or the door struck on the figure, but the starlight was enough for Jimmy. The height, the bulk of the shoulders, the slight angle to the side at which the head was carried, and the springing qualities of the walk all denoted The Streak.

And now he was passing up the broad steps to the veranda, now his step creaked on the boards of the veranda floor, now his silhouette appeared black against the doorway itself.

The Streak, standing like a hero at the mouth of the

ogre's cave. The Streak on the verge of the house of his enemies. It seemed to Jimmy that the stars were falling out of heaven in bewilderment. The earth whirled before Jimmy's eyes. For what could even The Streak accomplish in a place crowded with his enemies?

And yet—there was the squeak of the door as The Streak pushed it open.

Jimmy rose from his hiding and fled to the side of the saloon building. In a moment he was hanging like a monkey to the sill of an open window with the whole interior plainly before his eyes.

He never had had such a clear view of a saloon before. They are places forbidden to boys and everything that's important in the world takes place inside them. Whisky sours the air of a saloon and sweetens it, also. Whisky that burns the throat of a boy and sets the eyes of grown men on fire. Whisky that is the accompaniment of all the doings of the wise and the mature. Jimmy felt that he was looking in on a sort of reverend council chamber and duelling field combined, as he stared through the windows of Pete Reilly's saloon.

There was a good deal of smoke in the air. The ceiling was misted over, and from various cigarettes blue-brown wisps of smoke still were rising, making a strange writing in the air, all full of wavy lines, like the scribblings of an idiot.

Under those scribblings, those wavering exclamation points, sat men at the round tables, or else they stood along the bar. A dozen or fifteen men, and specially the black mustaches of Pete Reilly behind the bar.

He was leaning forward, his shoulders tilted, as he reached under the bar and gripped something. A gun, of course. In this position all his movement was arrested. And so were all the others in the saloon at a halt. They had their heads turned towards the door and not a man of them moved. Jimmy saw a long ash on the cigarette that was in the hand of big Jack Wheeler. The ash fell off and disappeared to powder on the floor, and still Jack Wheeler did not move or take his glance from the figure in the doorway.

That was The Streak. He stood there only for a moment, with his head high and a smile on his lips.

No other man in the world, Jimmy knew, could have stood there in the midst of his enemies, as The Streak was doing now.

The Streak said: "Hello, boys. Is Calico Charlie here with Shine?" No one answered. The Streak sauntered into the middle of the room and paused again.

"Any of you fellows tell me where I can find Calico Charlie and Shine?" he asked. He received no word.

Jimmy saw Tuck Waters move his right hand down towards the butt of his gun. The hand reached the butt, fingered it, and before Jimmy could cry out the warning, the hand had slipped on past the gun. It dangled harmlessly at the side of Waters.

Hugh Maskell moistened his lips and cleared his throat, as softly as though he were in church.

What would The Streak do now?

He walked straight on to the bar. Left and right, two men shrank back to give him more room. Their enchanted eyes stared at The Streak as though he were an unreal monster.

"Let me have one of those cold beers, Reilly, will you?" he asked.

It seemed to Jimmy the most wonderful speech that ever was made by a hero.

Reilly said: "Well—why, sure—why, sure, Streak!"

And he laughed a little. Reilly who hated The Streak so much. Reilly who had said that he would shoot down The Streak on sight if ever the outlaw dared to enter his saloon. Reilly who publicly had stated that the sawed-off shotgun underneath his bar would make up the difference between his skill and that of The Streak. Reilly now was trying to laugh, his mouth sagging open, his eyes huge, his face that of a fool.

"I'd rather die!" whispered Jimmy, sick with scorn.

Pete Reilly filled a blass and put it before The Streak. The hand of Reilly shook so much that the beer slopped over the edge of the glass. He started to mop up the beer and nudged the glass with the cloth and spilled more of the beer.

"That's all right," said The Streak. "I don't mind a wet deck, Reilly."

He was friendly. That's what he was. Friendly. In there among them all, and friendly!

The Streak said: "If any of you fellows want to go and tell Calico Charlie that I'm here, I'd be grateful. I want him and Shine! Will somebody try to find out where Calico Charlie may be?"

Waters said: "All right, I'll tell him."

Nobody else spoke but every man in the room turned and started for the door. And The Streak?

In that crisis, with all those enemies pouring into one solid mass, ready for battle, he did not even stir at the bar. He did not so much as turn his head to watch them and make sure of them. Perhaps that was because he had to keep Pete Reilly under his eye. But even Pete Reilly was not as dangerous as all the rest of them.

Two or three of the fellows nearing the door slowed up and glanced back, hesitant, watchful, towards The Streak, and then they went on.

It was very strange, until light struck suddenly across the brain of Jimmy. It was the big mirror behind the bar. That was the answer. In that mirror he could see the white-bandaged head of The Streak. And in that mirror, of course, The Streak could study all the rest of the room.

And they knew it, the cowards, and that was why they all swarmed on through the door.

One of them cried out, suddenly. They had flocked through too closely, there was a bit of a jam. Half a dozen voices shouted in unison. As though they expected the bullets of The Streak to strike them down as they were wedged there, helpless. Then they burst into the outer night, with a rush.

Would they turn in the darkness and fire through the open door? No, Jimmy could hear their footfalls scattering up and down the street.

CHAPTER 26

Conference

THE residence of Perry T. Baldwin had in former days simply been the "Baldwin House." When he put on the new porch with the tall white columns and built on the two wings, it became the "Baldwin Mansion," in the words of the Jasper *Journal*. In that mansion, Perry T. Baldwin had just finished saying good night to his wife before he went into his study.

He entered it in a darkness of thought for his wife's face was still in his mind. As a girl, she had had a pretty face, a sweet voice and manner, and five hundred acres that Baldwin needed. Now her face was brown and weary and puckered between the eyes. The spring was gone from her and a dry autumn had followed. As for the five hundred acres, he had had them so long that he no longer felt gratitude for them. Tonight he could see that he would have to make a change in wives.

She had been well enough for the old Jasper, but she would not do for the newer, greater town. She had fitted with the "Baldwin House," but she would not do at all for the "Baldwin Mansion." She did not fit in behind tall white columns. He could have possessed himself with patience if she had been in ill health, but as a matter of fact she was a tough, durable, lively woman. Therefore, divorce was the one way out. He would take, as a second wife, a woman with a distinguished presence and a good deal of money. Someone who understood how to sit at the head of a table and be gracious to guests.

She did not have to be very pretty but she had to have plenty of money. Because there were other projects than Jasper Valley that needed the developing hand of Perry T. Baldwin.

He was a man who made firm decisions and never varied from them. Now he made up his mind. In the morning, in the fresh of the day, firmly, kindly, he would

137

tell his wife of his decision. If she ventured something about the five hundred acres—well, he could show her certain vital signatures that she had written down those years ago. Like a good general, he had always planned every move with an eye to the future—preparing good lines of advance in case of victory, safe lines of retreat in case of defeat.

Rousing himself from his depth of thought, he started towards his desk, and it was then, for the first time, that he saw he had visitors, each with a gleam of white teeth grinning at him form the corner of the room. The seated figure was that of Calico Charlie. The vast bulk that stood behind Calico's chair was Shine, showing his fangs from ear to ear.

Baldwin said: "How are you, Calico?"

Calico, for answer, reached into a pocket and brought out the makings of a cigarette. He began to roll one without looking down at his work. His bland eyes remained fixed on the face of Baldwin as though he were considering words for his next speech.

"You didn't come in through the front door," said Baldwin. "Did you use the kitchen way?"

Calico hooked a thumb in the direction of the window. Baldwin nodded.

"What have you been doing, Calico?" he asked. "The people are buzzing about, a good deal. It's said that The Streak has you beaten. People say that you've met your master at last, Calico. But I don't feel that, of course."

"The boss has gotta leave Jasper Valley, Mr. Baldwin," said Shine.

"Leave Jasper Valley?" snapped Baldwin. "Calico, I've paid you a very considerable advance for the work that you were to do."

There was a little pause. Instead of answering, Calico lighted his cigarette, always thoughtful.

Shine said: "The work ain't here to do, no more, Mr. Baldwin."

"Not here? Why not here?" asked Baldwin. "The Streak is still alive and well."

"He's alive," said Shine. "But he ain't well, sir. He's mighty sick."

"How sick?" asked Baldwin.

"Sick in the head, sir," said Shine. "The boss met up with him and just took and slammed him over the head and kicked him in the face. And that was all the trouble he had with The Streak."

"You mean that you had him—like that—in your hands?" asked Baldwin. "And you let him get away?"

"There was a kind of mix up about a horse, sir," said Shine. "And The Streak got away. That's a good name for him. Streak. He sure streaked it when he got a chance to run. He didn't run for Calico. No, sir, he ran the other way fast as his legs would step. He's kept on running. You'll never see him in Jasper Valley again. He ain't got no more interest in this town, Mr. Baldwin."

"You think that you've run him out of the valley for good?" asked Baldwin.

"Yes, sir. We think so, the both of us," said Shine.

"I wish you'd speak for yourself, Calico," said Baldwin. Calico removed the cigarette from under his long white teeth and said, with his smile: "Why?"

Then he went on smoking, his eyes waiting for Baldwin's answer like the eyes of a patient child.

Baldwin said: "To run him out of the valley isn't enough—that's a peril to humanity. A man who is a natural murderer. He must die. Calico. Besides, he must die before you can claim the reward."

"The boss just wants to know where he's apt to find The Streak," said Shine. "That's all he wants to know. There's a whole lot of places where a bird can fly to from the middle of the sky. You know any place where The Streak would be likely to go? Like friends he might have, somewheres, while he lies in and lets his head get well?"

"He's been injured, has he?" demanded Baldwin.

"If he ain't got a rubber head, it sure would have been cracked," said Shine. "The boss, he hit that white man so hard that the doggone gun it fair jumped off the head of The Streak. It just kind of bounced off of his skull. The butt of that gun it made such a soggy kind of a sound, it seemed to sink right in, and the blood it come running dawn over his face.

"I had to kind of laugh. And the boss he up and kicks

that Streak right in the chin and flops him flat on his back, like you would of laughed to see it."

Here Shine set the good example by laughing shrill and high, with a wheeze in the sound like the neigh of a horse. Baldwin looked eagerly at the Negro and then shook his head.

"It doesn't seem possible," he said. "You had The Streak in your hands and yet you let him get away? You let ten thousand dollars walk right out of your path? Is that possible, Shine?"

"It was just one of those funny things, Mr. Baldwin," said Shine. "You wouldn't think that a horse could act up enough to get in the way of Calico Charlie, but a horse sure enough did that thing. You gunna be able to tell us, Mr. Baldwin, where we gunna go looking for that white man?"

"I don't know his past," said Baldwin. "It has jails and murder enough in it, I suppose, but I haven't been able to run down anything. I've had police inquiries made, and still we've found out nothing. But I'm to believe that The Streak really has been tried and found wanting? I'm to believe that he's been beaten down—and not with bullets?"

"There weren't no chance for the bullets," said Shine. "Because the boss got the drop so quick and so close onto The Streak, that the whole thing was over right away."

"I'm going to believe you," said Baldwin, frowning. "It's hard, but I'm going to believe you. And in the meantime, we'll try to spot his out-trail from Jasper. But The Streak on the run—on the run—beaten down with a gun-butt."

"Yellow," said Calico.

"Yellow?" echoed Baldwin, staring again.

"Yellow," said Calico, from his long white teeth. He pointed at the window again. "You keep watching. Why?"

"When we come here," broke in Shine, grinning, "we seen a man sort of walking around from bush to bush in the garden and always watching that house over there on the hill. The Coles house. And it seemed to the boss like it was a funny thing that you'd be watching the Coles house night and day. What would that be for? That's what the boss wanted to know."

"Watching the Coles house? Why should I hire a man

to watch the Coles house?" demanded Baldwin. "As a matter of fact, I have to keep a guard near my house because there are some brutally rough characters in Jasper Valley, my friends, and there are fools who hold a grudge against me because I did not encourage the building of the new station in the center of Jasper. Fools who cannot see that there will be a greater Jasper in the time to come. On account of people of that caliber, I have to keep a guard over my house. If the fellow you watched was staring at the Coles house, I dare say it because he was interested in it on his own account."

"All right," said Calico, with his white flash of a smile.

Footfalls ran up the veranda of the Baldwin house and a hand banged heavily at the front door.

Only a moment later, some one hurried to the study door and tapped excitedly on it.

"Come in!" called Baldwin. The door was pushed open a little by a servant who said: "There's people here to see you, Mr. Baldwin. The Streak is—The Streak—"

"The Streak?" exclaimed Baldwin. "The Streak? Show those people in!"

He turned and stared at Calico, who was rising slowly to his feet.

Half a dozen men were crowding through the door of the study, now, and Baldwin exclaimed: "What is it?"

There was a general outburst, a roar of sound with nothing clearly audible except the name: "The Streak!"

"You tell me, Waters," said Baldwin. "The rest of them seem to be half out of their heads."

"Right here in the town—right here in Jasper—in Pete Reilly's saloon," cried Waters. "The Streak walked right in on us."

He pointed his hand at Calico Charlie.

"He wants Calico Charlie!" cried Waters. "He wants to get at Calico and Shine before morning. He's on a rampage and he's gunna do his murders right this here night!"

Perry T. Baldwin, saying nothing, turned and fixed his eyes steadily upon Calico Charlie. The latter said, simply: "Where?"

"Pete Reilly's saloon," said Waters.

"Show me," said Calico Charlie.

CHAPTER 27

At Pete Reilly's Saloon

WELL before that odd night visit of Calico to the house of Perty T. Baldwin, Jimmy had run across the street from Pete Reilly's saloon to more friendly quarters; and, in spite of his youth, he knocked open the swing doors of Flynn's and ran straight in. For it would be strange if there were not friends of The Streak present at that place.

"Hey!" shouted fat Mr. Flynn. "You take and get out of here, Jimmy. What you mean sashayin' into my saloon this time of night? You go and fetch yourself out of here!"

Instead of retreating, Jimmy stared about the room and at once saw at a corner table the chunky shoulders of Buck McGuire and the long neck and long, lean face of Bill Roan. He made straight for their table. There were other men in the room. There was big Harry Layden, for instance, up near the bar. But Bill Roan and Buck McGuire, those admitted friends of The Streak, who had known him in the old days, were by all odds the sort of people that Jimmy wanted to see just then. So he ran to their table and without greeting burst forth in a voice that could be heard all through the room: "The Streak! The Streak! He's over at Pete Reilly's. He's cleaned out the place. He's gone and sent everybody to go and look for Charlie."

"He'd better look for the devil in the hottest part of hell fire," said Buck McGuire. "What does he want with Calico charlie? Where is he? Reilly's? We'll go and take a look."

Harry Layden had heard, also, and he came with great strides that shook the floor.

He said to Bill Roan: "What do you fellows want? To hold up The Streak, or just stand by and see him fall?"

No one answered him. They poured out onto the

142

street. The dust rolled up in heavy, stifling volumes as they hurried across to Pete Reilly's saloon.

Behind the bar stood Pete, his face polished red with perspiration, his hands gripped together, his eyes staring with a permanent terror.

The Streak was merely saying: "You took the wrong attitude, Reilly. You were all right. It was just your beer that I didn't like. Why hate me because I didn't love your beer?"

Pete Reilly sagged his lower jaw and mumbled: "Sure. You're right. You're right, Streak."

Then the muttering of footfalls across the veranda and into the saloon caused The Streak to straighten, looking into the bar mirror. Afterwards, he spun about on his heel.

"*Hai,* Jimmy!" he said. "What you doing up this late at night?"

It was one of those deathless moments. Out of four, and three of them adult friends, The Streak had chosen Jimmy for his first salutation.

Afterwards, he said: "*Hai,* Harry—Buck, you come around to read me a lecture?"

Bill Roan pointed a finger at the bartender.

"Get busy back stage, brother," he said. "We don't need you or your beer for a minute, you fat-faced son of bad luck."

Pete Reilly turned with a groan of relief and disappeared.

Buck said: "Now what you aim to do, you damn fool? . . . I mean *asking* for Calico?"

"I'm staying here," said Blondy, and clapped a kindly hand on the shoulder of Buck. "Jimmy, you go home . . . If you won't go home, step outside and tell us when the crowd heaves in sight, will you?"

"Sure I will," said Jimmy.

He remained for a half second, filling his eyes with the sight of the hero, and then he went out of the room with one hand pressed to his head, an instinctive gesture that sympathized with the bandage about the brows of The Streak. To Jimmy, no golden crown of empire was ever half so glorious as that white circlet, with the little stain of red creeping through the cloth above the temple.

"There's gunna be hell. Get out of here," said Buck. "You come along with us, kid."

"I'm staying," said Blondy.

"He's staying," interpreted Bill Roan, his mouth agape.

"Yeah," muttered Buck. "I heard him say so."

A silence drifted over the three of them. Then Blondy remarked: "When they come, they'll come in a herd. They won't be particular who they get under their hoofs, either. Bill, you and Buck vamoose out of here. Sashay right out of Jasper. It's not going to be a good place for my friends, after tonight."

"And what happens to you?" asked Buck, snarling out the words.

"I have a little party of my own. That's all," answered Blondy.

"You're gunna wait here—with an empty gun?" asked Buck.

"No. I've got five slugs in it, now."

"What good'll that do, when you can't hit nothing but a phonograph?" demanded Bill Roan.

"I can make a little noise, anyway," said Blondy. "Boys, you slope along."

"What's come over him?" asked Buck of Bill Roan. "What's happened to the kid? He means it!"

"He don't care," said Bill Roan. "He don't care about nothing. Wouldn't that damn you? Kid, why won't you hit the breeze?"

"I can't leave Jasper Valley," said Blondy.

"You like the idea they got about you here? You like it well enough to die for it?" demanded Buck.

"Well—put it that way," said Blondy.

"Now listen to me, Dummy—" began Bill Roan.

"Shut up, Bill," said Buck McGuire. "It ain't any good. The kid's made up his mind. He doggone near *wants* to die! Only thing is, can we get Perry T. Baldwin to call off the dogs?"

"It's no good," answered Blondy. "He's as deep in this game as a fly in Tanglefoot. There was something between him and Coles. That's the answer. They were better friends than people think."

"A bird like Perry T. Baldwin," said Bill Roan, "ain't friends with nobody but himself. And he's only friendly with himself on Sundays and holidays. What makes you say he liked Coles?"

"So much," said Blondy, "that he goes down to the Coles house now and works in his spare time to straighten up the affairs of Coles—works in the library—hunting through books for things that will tie up the loose ends of Coles's affairs. Is that friendship, I ask you—and for a man that's dead?"

"When you see him doing that?"

"Mary Layden saw him, tonight—going through the library books of Coles, one by one, shaking the leaves of them, trying to find things."

"Who said it was friendship to search a dead man's library?" demanded Bill Roan.

"And by night, too," broke in Buck.

"With all that front he's got, is Perry T. Baldwin just a rat?" demanded Bill Roan. "I begin to think he is. Blondy, we're all three gunna go up to the Coles house."

"Yeah," sighed Buck. "We're gunna go up. The first time I was in that cemetery, I knew that I'd have to be there again. We're going to the Coles house."

"Why?" demanded Blondy.

"To find out what Baldwin was looking for," explained Bill Roan. "Don't be dumb, Blondy. Try to be a little brighter in the pinches. You coming along?"

"I suppose I will," said Blondy. "I set the stage for something to happen. I asked Calico down here to have it out. And now I suppose that I'll slide out on him like a dirty gray rat. No, I'm going to stay right here, Bill. Nothing has ever happened. Nothing but talk has happened in Jasper Valley so far as I'm concerned. But tonight something *is* going to happen. I'm meeting Calico Charlie. And I'm meeting him here."

To this quiet announcement, Bill Roan and Buck listened with startled eyes. Buck pointed. "Nothing happens to you?" he demanded. "Where you get that bandage around your bean?"

"When I left you boys, I went back to the barn in the woods. To pick up a few things. Calico found me there and slammed me with the butt of his gun. That's all."

"Yeah? Go on!" exclaimed Bill Roan. "And then—?"

"There's no use talking about it," said Blondy. "If I start talking about it, you'll think like everybody else in Jasper Valley that I'm able to do big things. You'll begin to think that I'm something more than the worst cowpuncher that ever tried to daub a rope on a cow. The fact is that Rocket got mixed into the game; and in the fuss that followed I was able to run for my life. That's all there was to it. Nothing happened, again."

The voice of Jimmy panted, at the door: "Streak, there's a whole mob coming! It ain't right for you to wait for a whole mob! You'd be killing too many that are only bad once in a while. . . ."

The footfalls of Jimmy ran down the veranda steps again.

"Well, I'll go along with you," said Blondy heavily.

CHAPTER 28

Tenner's Signal

THEY were back among the trees of the side alley when the mob came pouring towards Pete Reilly's saloon. They could hear Pete's voice saying: "Some of you get around behind the house. This is gunna be the end of him. The Streak's gunna finish up this same night! Calico, you can have the entrance by the front door all to yourself!"

Jimmy had joined the three the instant they left the saloon. And now he muttered: "It's mighty fine of you, Streak, to come away just because I asked you to. I mean, how many of 'em would you do in when they're as thick as flies, this way? You'd have the dust all wet down with their blood."

"Jimmy, you do something for me, will you?"

"Sure. Anything."

"Promise?"

"Yeah. Promise anything."

"Go home to bed."

"I can't do that, Streak. I'd die if I went home and laid down."

"I've got your promise."

A long, whispering sigh passed the lips of Jimmy.

"All right," he said. "All right . . . I'll go . . . so long, Streak."

He stood still, and they walked away from him.

They started across up the winding lanes that lay behind Reilly's and headed toward Coles's house. They came near the house and Blondy and Harry Layden went quietly along the side of it and stole up onto the back porch one after the other, lest the weight of both on a single board might cause it to creak too loudly.

Each took his stand on a side of the screen door.

A door in front of the house suddenly banged. A voice called out. "That's Buck," said Blondy. "And he's pretty hot."

Then they heard the mutter of someone approaching on the run. And rapidly the footfalls swept into the rear of the house.

"Use your fist!" said Harry.

"Hands," cautioned Blondy, "or else you'll break him in two."

The kitchen door jerked open. The screen was flung back into the face of Blondy. He reached past it. It was as though he had caught at a snake that wriggled instantly out of his grasp. Through the surer grasp of Harry Layden, also, the fugitive slipped and sprang down the steps.

A great shadow hurled after him. That was Harry Layden jumping. If he missed, in that headlong leap, he would smash bones on the hard ground beneath. But he did not miss. He landed on the fleeing silhouette. There was a gasp. Then Layden stood up, dragging something with him.

"I've got him," said Layden. "It's Tenner, too."

Buck and Bill Roan, on the sprint, hurtled around the side of the house.

"I've got him!" called Harry Layden.

"I told you what he'd do," said Bill Roan. "And he wouldn't of run, either, unless he was afraid that we could get something out of him that was worth having. Haul him inside, and we'll have a light!"

"Where's the library?" asked Buck of Tenner.

"Inside," said Tenner.

They passed in through the kitchen door. And Blondy lighted a match which showed him a lamp on the table near the sink. He touched the flame to the wick and pushed the chimney back into place.

The room was in flawless order. The oilcloth on top of the table shone like checkered marble; the floor was scrubbed white; the stove glistened with new polish.

Tenner was saying: "Now, gentlemen, it don't matter what you do; I guess you're all gonna do time for burglary. Forcing your way into a residence—"

Blondy walked up to him and tapped a forefinger on the hollow chest: "If we're willing to do burglary, it means that we're here for business," he said. "Now you show us the library."

"Bah!" said Tenner. "Find your own way—and all be damned! You're breaking my shoulder with those damned hands of yours, Mr. Layden. Burglary and physical violence. They send 'em up for twenty years, for things like that."

"What'll I do to him?" asked Layden. "How'll we make him talk?"

"Give his hair a twist; yank the scalp off him," suggested Buck.

"Let him alone," commanded Blondy.

He looked into the faces of his three friends with a curious wonder. Physical violence was not the thing to use on Tenner. Just what the proper method was he could not tell. But torment of the body was not the way for one who had passed through so much spiritual hell. He watched the mouth of Tenner twisting between a sneer and an attempt at courageous smiling to show his contempt for danger.

"We can find the library, well enough," said Blondy.

He led the way with the lamp, opening doors right and left down the hall. Already there was in the air of the vacant house a queer smell of dust and damp. The entire front part of it was untouched by the care of Tenner. To the kitchen alone he confined his housekeeping.

Then, on the left, he pushed open the door that gave them a glimpse of the rows of books running around and around a big room. The shelves were broken into by two large windows.

Bill Roan ordered Tenner to sit in a chair. When he had been placed in it, with the big hands of Harry Layden nearby to keep him in order, Bill Roan said: "Now, what does Perry T. Baldwin come snooping up around here at night for?"

Tenner dropped his head against the back of the chair and closed his eyes. He smiled.

Buck came up and actually dropped upon one knee, in the strength of his earnestness.

He stabbed at Tenner with a hard forefinger, saying: "Listen, Tenner. There's a mob up in Jasper. They want The Streak for the killing of Coles. The Streak didn't kill Coles. Who did?"

Tenner shrugged his shoulders. There was nothing but excited pleasure in his white face.

He kept his eyes closed.

It seemed to Blondy that the man liked this physical disturbance.

"We're taking it easy to start with," announced Bill Roan. "But we ain't gunna keep our hands away from you too long. Listen, Tenner, you got no more rights with us than a gray rat would have in a family of cats. Understand? In a family of cats! We're gunna break you up so small that you'll digest dead easy, unless you talk."

Tenner remained silent. The smile did not leave his face. His eyes would not open. It was plain, to Blondy, that the man was deriving the most exquisite pleasure from this moment of physical danger.

"Let's begin on him," suggested Harry Layden. "As long as there's dirty work to do, let's get it over. How'll we start, Buck? What'll we do to him?"

"Get some slivers off that wood by the fireplace and shove the splinters up under his finger nails," said Buck. "Ever happen to ram a splinter up under a fingernail when you were carpentering around?"

Bill Roan, without a word, went to the hearth and from the rough sides of some split wood which was piled in the basket, snapped off a number of the ragged splinters. He came back with them in his hand.

"We hate to do this rotten job," said Bill Roan. "But

we sure gotta make you talk. Tenner, you know who killed
Coles. Everybody in town says that you know. You come
out with it and tell us; or else you get everything that we
can give you."

Tenner laughed. The sound was a mere panting with,
somewhere inside, a sort of shrill whining. The laughter
ended. He licked the gray of his thin lips. His eyes remained closed.

"I'm giving you a last chance," said Bill Roan. "Who
killed Philip B. Coles?"

"The Streak!" said Tenner.

Three heads jerked. Three pairs of eyes stared suddenly
at Blondy.

He felt a dash of cold against his face, through his
blood.

Tenner, opening his eyes for the first time, looked
brightly, hungrily about him.

"Lying—you think lying will get you out?" demanded
Harry Layden.

"How d'you know?" asked Tenner, leaning a little
forward in his chair. "How d'you know that The Streak
didn't do it?"

"I know it inside my heart," said Harry Layden.

"Oh, your heart, eh?" repeated Tenner. "Philip B.
Coles—he had a heart, too!" His laughter came again,
the same horrible caricature.

"Start in on him," said Buck. "He ain't human. *I'll* do
the starting. Give me them splinters, Bill."

Bill Roan, his disgusted eyes profoundly fixed on Tenner, handed over the splinters. But Blondy said: "Hold
on, boys. Tenner, tell me how you know that I killed
Coles."

"You walked right through the front door, because
Coles had signaled you to come up. From his window he
done the signaling," said Tenner. "You didn't see me,
but I seen you from down the hallway. I seen you look
around as you came in. Then I seen you fetch out a gun
and give it a look before you put it away again.

"You went up the stairs, and you didn't know that I was
slipping over the carpet behind you, making a catwalk
out of it, and no sound. I stood right outside of the door.
I stood there and I heard you talk. I heard you damning

Philip B. Coles, and I heard him tryin' to explain. I heard him whining, and trying to explain."

"What was he trying to explain?" asked Blondy.

"About the money he was to have paid you for a job you done."

"What job?" asked Blondy.

"A killing job. I don't know who it was that you killed."

"What did Coles say, exactly?"

"Leave me close the windows," said Tenner, "and then I'll tell you. I'll catch a chill."

"We'll go and shut 'em for you, Tenner," said Blondy.

"You can't; they work on a catch I can hardly handle myself," said Tenner.

He rose from the chair and picked up the lamp. At the first window he struggled a moment with the catch, then pulled down the sash.

At the second he delayed a little longer, and the lamp in his hand raised, lowered, then swayed from side to side, describing a cross before Tenner succeeded in closing the window pane.

CHAPTER 29

Parley

THE statement of Tenner had left Bill Roan and Buck McGuire uncertainly glowering at Blondy. It had a totally different effect on Harry Layden. He had turned a deep crimson and his hands opened and shut like two pairs of jaws, eager to be tearing prey.

"There's four of us here," said Harry Layden, "and all that we can do with ourselves is to stand around and listen to this dirty dog tell lies about The Streak. What's the matter with you fellows?"

Tenner had returned to his chair. Blondy had drawn down the window shades.

At once the room grew still and warm. Perspiration started on the body.

Blondy pulled up a chair facing that of Tenner and sat

down on the edge of it. He tried to fasten on the eyes of
Tenner, but those eyes kept writhing and shifting out of
the attention that was fixed upon them. It seemed that
Tenner, in the center of the stage, wanted to keep watching the effect he made on the others in the room.

Blondy said: "You stood outside the door and heard the
talk, did you?"

"Yeah. I said that," answered Tenner, with his sneer.

"Why don't you loosen up and tell us some of it?
How long were you outside the door before the shot was
fired—by me?" asked Blondy.

"I was there a long time. Maybe a couple of minutes,"
said Tenner.

"And all the time I was asking for the money that
Coles owed me—for a killing?"

"That's right," said Tenner. "It wasn't the cash, really.
You know that. You wanted back your card."

"What card?" asked Blondy.

"Yeah. You talk as though you don't know," said
Tenner.

He half rose and shook his fist in the face of Blondy,
"You wanted back your card out of the file . . . the card
that showed how much money you owed to Coles."

"He loaned me money, did he?" asked Blondy.

"Yes, he loaned you money. You damn well know that
he loaned you money."

Bill Roan said, slowly: "This is hell. Why d'you want
to keep on talking to him, Blondy? You like to have
the dirt throwed in your face?"

Tenner said: "You told him that he'd sucked blood
long enough and that he wasn't going to fatten on your
life."

Blondy, leaning forward still, kept his intent gaze fixed
on the brillant, shifting eyes of Tenner.

"You knew all this, and you didn't tell it to anybody?"
asked Blondy.

"I told it to one man," said Tenner.

"Who was that?"

"The only man that stands up strong for law and order
in Jasper!" said Tenner. "I told it to Perry T. Baldwin."

"D'you see the picture, boys?" asked Blondy. He turned
towards his friends. But even the faith of Harry Layden

seemed to be badly shaken by this time. He stared down moodily at the floor.

Then Blondy asked: "Coles was a business man, wasn't he? Wasn't he a business man, Tenner?"

"He was nothing *but* business," said Tenner.

"Then what a fool he was to lend money to me!" said Blondy. "What a half-witted fellow he was to lend money to me, when I had no security to offer him outside of a *horse and saddle!*"

The eyes of Tenner turned suddenly blank. "How do I know how you got the loan?" he demanded. "Maybe it was at the point of your gun."

"Do you hear that, boys?" asked Blondy. "At the point of a gun I get money out of Coles and then I sign a promissory note to pay back the money I get with a gun. Does that make sense?"

"No!" shouted Harry Layden. "It don't make sense. No sense at all. I knew Tenner was lying all the way through."

"He didn't lie all the way through," said Blondy. "He told his yarn with too much feeling. I think he *did* stand outside the door and listen to Coles talking with the fellow who finally murdered him. I think the murderer *was* a man who owed money to Coles. And while the talk went on, Tenner stood outside the door and licked his chops and rubbed his hands together. Tenner, when they stand you up in court and ask why you didn't yell out, or try to get into the room, what will you say?"

"I was too scared," said Tenner.

"You could have run downstairs and started shouting. That would have scared the murderer away before he did his stuff," said Blondy. "Why didn't you do that? Why did you just stand there?"

Tenner paused. In the pause, for the first time the small beads of perspiration varnished his pale face.

Blondy said: "Was it because you knew the voice of the man inside the room there with Coles?"

Tenner was confused and he remained silent.

"He won't talk," said Buck, "because he's sold out. Whoever he heard talking with Coles has got enough hard cash to buy out Tenner and keep his mouth shut. I wonder what God thinks of himself, putting this kind of a self-poisoning snake on the ground and calling it a man?"

Here the eyes of Tenner lifted and shifted, suddenly. And a moment later they all heard it—the creaking of the springs of the screen door at the rear of the house, and then the muffled treading of many feet, a sense of moving weight rather than actual trampling on the floor.

"The front way!" said Bill Roan. "Make it fast, old sons. There's trouble gumshoeing up behind us!"

There was no need to start. Someone sneezed in the front hall and they distinctly heard a warning murmur of many voices. Buck slipped noiselessly to the door and turned the lock in it.

"The windows!" he whispered over his shoulder.

Tall Bill Roan already was at a window, gradually lifting the shade, working it so that it might run noiselessly on its roller. But it hardly had risen an inch before a gunshot boomed outside the house. Bill Roan jumped back. A thin tinkling of falling glass rained down in the second of silence. Blondy saw a little round hole bored through the shade. Not little, either, if it were slipped through the body of a living man.

In that small interval, not longer than one stroke of the heart, Blondy looked around him and saw the faces of his friends. They were brave, all of them, he knew; but they were not ready to die. The eyes of Harry Layden stared at a bodiless nightmare of dread. Bill Roan had bent over a little as though a fist had been buried in that long, lean body of his. And Buck McGuire's face was twisted all to one side by a very sour taste. Tenner, instead, gripping both arms of his chair, sat there with his mouth open, grinning, as though he were about to burst into song.

And then the crash came—a whole choir of voices breaking out with a roar from both sides and the front of the house. Voices sounding sharp and far outside the house, and a chorus booming and muffled with self-made echoes inside the Coles house itself.

CHAPTER 30

No Escape

THAT first uproar died away but was not finished when Tenner screeched out, sharp as a crowing rooster: "He's in here and three friends with him—McGuire—Harry Layden—and Bill Roan."

Layden reached the flat of a big hand at Tenner, and Tenner curled up in the chair with his hands in front of his face and his knees raised, like a cat that falls on its back before fighting. He was silent, but laughing like a silent devil at all of them. A hand wrenched the knob of the library door. Then came a heavy knocking.

The voice of Perry T. Baldwin himself called out: "Are you there, Tenner?"

Tenner started to answer, but shrank from the raised hand of Layden. Blondy called out: "I'm in here, Baldwin. Tenner's here. And the other three that Tenner named. They'll come out with their hands in the air if you'll promise that no harm comes to them."

"We want you. Damn the rest," said Baldwin. "Let them come out. No one cares what happens to them."

Tenner pointed his scrawny arm at Blondy and said: "You're the sinking ship. Now the rats'll leave you, Streak. And when you go down, remember that *I* did it. *I* sent 'em the signal through the window with the lamp. *I* did it, and nobody else!"

Blondy held out his hand, muttering: "So long, boys. You stuck by me as long as you could. But your money is no good now. I'm the only one who can pay for all this music."

Buck took hold of the hand. He leaned close, peering into the eyes of Blondy. "How do you feel, kid?" he asked.

"Tired," said Blondy, smiling a little.

He could not help smiling to see the terrible tenseness of Buck, the stiff tremor of the lips. Because Buck was like the rest of them. They wanted to live. They did not need to die because luck had not stacked the cards against them and the world never would ask from them more than they had to give. They never had seen a woman's face grow white and cold with scorn.

So Blondy smiled. He had told the perfect truth. He was simply tired. And the whole thing soon would be over. There is room enough in a half-inch bullet hole for a human soul to spread wings and fly.

Buck turned abruptly away: "The rest of you get out," he said. "If the kid can take it this way, I can take it the same. If I double-crossed him before, I can go straight with him now."

"You talk like a damn fool," said Bill Roan. "I ain't done any work for a couple of day, and I kind of need exercise."

Harry Layden said: "I'm scared to death. If I don't look it, then faces lie. But where you stick, I stick, Streak."

"Ah, my God," said Blondy, "do I have to argue with you about it?"

Tenner snarled: "It's all a fake. It's all a bluff. The minute the guns start talking, you'll all yell for help. There ain't *any* man that could keep his friends in a pinch like this."

They could hear Perry T. Baldwin giving instructions in his loud voice in the hall, telling some to fall back and give plenty of clearance around the door, ordering others to double the watch over the windows outside the house.

Now he shouted: "We're ready to have you out of that room. Do you come with 'em, Streak, with your hands over your head?"

"I'll stay here, Baldwin," said The Streak. "But will you listen to me? There are three halfwits in here who refuse to leave me. What can be done about 'em?"

"Stay with you?" cried Baldwin. "Stay in *there* with you?"

"They won't budge," said Blondy.

The voice of Perry T. Baldwin repeated, distantly as he turned from the door: "They won't get out of the room—Roan, McGuire and young Layden. What about that, sheriff?"

Sheriff Wallace Nash distinctly answered: "If a piece of meat wants to stew in the soup, you can't get it out except you burn your fingers. Why would you want to burn your fingers about the three in there? Harry Layden was never no good, much, and the other two are strangers."

Baldwin said: "Have I the legal right to go ahead and blast a way into that room, regardless of what happens to any of the people inside it?"

"*You* haven't," answered Sheriff Nash. "But I have. And what you're doing now is with my sanction, Baldwin."

"The dirty dog!" said Harry Layden.

"You see how it is," said Blondy. "They'll cut right in through the three of you. Will you get out of this room?"

"Why talk, Blondy?" asked Bill Roan. "We're all gunna stick— Kind of somehow my mind goes back to a tune. You remember 'The Trail to Arkansas'? It sure started us trailing high, wide and handsome."

Baldwin's voice thundered, suddenly: "I'm making the last call. If any of you will come out, well and good. If not, we start shooting through the doors and windows; we smash them in and when we get at you we get at you in earnest. You understand me?"

Here Tenner screamed out: "Mr. Baldwin! Mr. Baldwin! You ain't going to shoot into the room while I'm here, are you?"

"Tenner, I want to take care of you," said Baldwin. "I intend to take care of you, but in the name of the law and uprightness in Jasper Valley, we have to get The Streak . . . Calico, are you ready?"

Tenner went towards the door in a sort of dancing ecstasy. He screamed: "Mr. Baldwin, damn the law and uprightness—you're gunna get me murdered! Mr. Baldwin—"

"Open up!" cried Baldwin from the hallway.

A blast roared from the hall and hit the door. The heavy wood sagged and crackled under the impact of the bullets. Bill Roan pulled a gun and fired three times, yelling out: "*Hai*, Baldy! *Hai*, damn your old sides! *Hai*, Baldy."

He had gone back to mule-driving in that high emergency. Wherever his bullets traveled, they came close enough to make small trouble. The firing ended suddenly. Someone was cursing in a high-pitched voice that sounded almost like a woman protesting.

And Perry T. Baldwin could be heard saying: "I think that's enough. We can knock down the door with a rush, now. It's weakened enough by this time."

Tenner, as though the uproar of the bullets had dazed him, had remained after the first volley right in front of the door, with both hands clasped to his face. Now, in the silence, he uttered a cry that had no words in it, and turned slowly about.

Blood was bursting through the fingers of his hands and streaming down over his clothes. Blondy went to him and pulled the hands away from that frightful face. He had been shot through both cheeks. When he tried to speak, blood and shattered teeth spouted out and fell on the floor.

Blondy pulled out a bandanna.

"Stuff this inside your mouth," he directed. "That'll stop the bleeding inside, I think. We'll tie something else around on the outside—and get you out of here—"

"He don't get out," said Bill Roan. "He goes to hell with us, like a label."

Blondy already was stuffing the bandanna inside the red-streaming, gaping mouth. He took hold of the coat of Tenner, ripped it off, and then tore the man's shirt literally from his back. With that he made a clumsy bandage and tied it around the head of Tenner. But it could not stop the bleeding altogether. Tenner, like a child at gaze, held up his hand, and from under the swathing bandage he caught the blood that dripped down from his chin. And then he looked downwards helplessly at the pool of red that formed in the palm of his hand.

And all the while the loud, ringing voice of Perry T. Baldwin went on giving orders in the hall.

"Break down the newel post of the stairs, there. The newel post is the post at the foot of the balustrade."

A loud grinding and ripping noise answered that command.

"Well done, boys!" called Baldwin. "Now three or four of you take that post and smash in the library door. We'll have this rat-den cleared out all in a moment."

Someone answered: "The Streak's inside there. The first three or four that try to get through that door are gunna be dead men, Mr. Baldwin."

"We have Calico Charlie here to checkmate The Streak," said Baldwin.

"Now, here's the funny thing," drawled Bill Roan, inside the library: "Why should that Baldwin be so dead set agin you, Blondy? When did you ever slap him in the face?"

"I never touched him. Hardly knew him," said Blondy. "Look here. We can't let this Tenner bleed to death."

"Why not?" asked Harry Layden. "He put us in this pickle. Damn him, he closed the trap on all of us. Let him stew till he chokes."

As though the word represented the truth, Tenner tore the stifling gag from his mouth. A rush of blood followed it and poured down over his coat, already dripping red. He tried to talk. Wordless noises alone issued from his throat. Blondy put a hand before his eyes to shut out the image and yet he had to jerk the hand down again to watch. Tenner was stumbling towards the door, making with both hands appealing gestures for freedom.

Blondy shouted: "Baldwin! Baldwin! Are you there?"

"There's The Streak now," said Baldwin. "You'll see the real stuff he's made of. Listen to him beg!"

"We're going to open the door," said Blondy, "and let Tenner out, if you'll promise not to try to rush the door when he leaves. He's hurt."

"I make no promises!" roared Baldwin. "I don't make treaties with scoundrels like the pack of you."

"He's bleeding to death," said Blondy. "If he dies, you've murdered him, Baldwin."

Through that dialogue, Tenner stood close to the door, turning with extended hands of supplication first to one speaker and then to the other. A horrible, whining sobbing commenced in his throat when Baldwin made his refusal.

They could hear the Sheriff say: "I don't see what's the matter with that, Mr. Baldwin. By your account, it was Tenner that trapped 'em. If they're willing to let him go, why not take him and promise not to crowd 'em while the door is being opened and shut?"

Even after this there was a short pause, and Tenner, drawn erect and tense with expectation, shook his doubled fists over his head to hurl down curses on Baldwin.

At last Perry T. Baldwin announced: "We'll let you unlock the door and pass out Tenner, then. Go ahead with it, Streak."

Through the blood, as he stood wavering with shock and weakness, joy dawned strangely on the deformed face of Tenner.

"All right," said Blondy. "Come along, Tenner."

He took the key to the room from Buck and started towards the door. Harry Layden, shrugging his shoulders, turned his back on them. He did not see Tenner suddenly shake that bleeding head and point towards the closet door at the end of the room. He did not see Tenner start across the floor as rapidly as his shaking knees would permit him to go.

But Blondy, amazed, and Bill Roan behind him, followed Tenner as the latter pulled the door open.

The whole interior was lined with shelves on which papers were stacked in sheaves and bundles. Tenner gripped the sides of the range of shelves that faced the door and pulled it. He made a gesture as though to draw it away, and with both hands he made a sweeping movement to indicate that the others should pass on through the wall, as it were. Then he turned, shambling on towards the library door to the hall.

Blondy reached it before him and unlocked it. The two red hands of Tenner grasped one of Blondy's. The door yawned. The wounded man staggered out into the hallway. A chorus of astonished, horrified voices greeted him. Blondy closed the door and turned the lock again.

And he heard the sheriff saying: "What happened to you, man? . . . Where's the doctor? Where's the doctor? Get Doc Morrison, some of you. I've seen Morrison here, tonight."

But, inside the library, all four had now gathered at the closet to which Tenner had led the way.

"What's the fool mean?" asked Buck.

"He means that there's something worth having inside of those stacks of papers," said Harry Layden. "There might be a hundred million there, but all we want is to get out of this hell-hole."

"He means for us to get that stack of shelves out of the closet," answered Bill Roan. "Let's do it. Tenner is trying to pay us back for turning him loose. Lay hold, Harry."

They gripped the central section of the shelves. It came away bodily, for the load of papers which it carried was large but not heavy. They bore the shelves right out through the door and back into the library. It was clear away before they made out, behind it, a second unsuspected door let into the wall of the closet.

There was no handle to it. When Layden put his big hand against it, the door rattled gently against the bolt of its lock.

Blondy tried the key to the library. It fitted into the lock readily enough, but when he turned the key, it would not give.

"Break it down, then!" said Layden. "Tenner has showed us a way out."

"Break it down and the noise will tell the rest of 'em what we're doing," answered Bill Roan. "Don't be a fool all your life, Layden."

CHAPTER 31

No Surrender

As they stared at the door, as at a dumb face which might have spoken great words of knowledge, they could hear the voice of Perry T. Baldwin, muffled behind the wall at the other end of the room, as he shouted: "Bring up the newel post. That's right. Who'll volunteer to handle this? Any volunteers?"

Buck strode back down the room, raised his Colt, and drilled an extra hole through the door. Something heavy crashed on the floor of the hall. Footfalls stampeded away.

And Baldwin cried out: "Are you going to run like a

flock of rabbits? I want volunteers for handling this post. Come on, my lads. I'll take the first place. If anyone goes down, I'll be the man. That's right, Tomlinson! Good fellow. I knew I could count on you, Waters. Are you ready?"

Layden glanced once over his shoulder, frantically. Then he grasped the key of the closet door and turned with a desperate pressure. And the lock moved, with a faint, low, grinding sound as though to speak its reluctance. Once more Layden turned and this time the lock gave completely. A push of the hand thrust the sealed door open. They had before them darkness, the damp smell of a cellar, and the first steps of a descending flight of stairs.

There was no difficult explanation. Long before some remodeling of the house, the present library must have been the kitchen, and when the plan was altered, the cellar steps that originally led up to the old kitchen for the convenience of the cook had been left, as a matter of course, still connecting with what had once been the top landing of the stairs, but was now the library closet. Layden, with a small electric flashlight, suddenly probed the well. They saw the dingy steps go down to a brick flooring beneath.

"Buck!" called Blondy softly. Buck came swiftly. Layden already was passing down the steps with the torch in one hand and his gun in the other. Behind him followed Bill Roan. Blondy waited for Buck to pass through before him, and as Buck reached the head of the stairs, Baldwin's voice shouted in the distance—feet rushed—the door of the library went to pieces with a crash and the shattered bits of it rattled inwards on the library floor.

The force of that lunging impact brought all the four who had carried the newel post rushing and stumbling into the library. Baldwin himself, in the front place, stumbled on the doorsill and fell at full length, rolling over and over.

And Blondy saw the fall, and the pile up of the other bearers of the battering-ram. He had a wild desire to turn and start throwing lead into that pile of arms and waving legs. But another sight changed his mind. For the slight figure of Calico Charlie dodged into the room im-

mediately behind the bearers of the ram and came instantly towards the gaping entrance of the closet. The little
fellow ran like a snipe that dodges in the air, footing it
swiftly against the wind. Behind him loomed Shine, laughing, his rubbery face stretching into a new shape.

Blondy had one glimpse of the pair of them as he
slammed the door to the cellar stairs. He turned the latch
of the lock. That should delay them a priceless second or
two.

Then a red hot iron plunged through the left leg of
Blondy, high up between the knee and the hip. The bark
of the gun boomed in his ear at the same moment, seeming
very far away.

"All right, Blondy?" called Harry Layden, far ahead.

"All right, Harry!" shouted Blondy.

He tried to make a step. His left leg had no strength,
no purpose in it. It doubled and pitched him down on
his knee. It was numb, asleep.

He could hear Bill Roan saying: "When we get through
the cellar door, each man take his own line. Left, right
and straight ahead. Mind that, Blondy!"

They thought he was up there with them. The slant
door of the cellar banged open suddenly. A moment
later guns outside of the house were roaring. And then
men shouting, cursing.

What luck had the besiegers had shooting by dim
lamplight at three men making a breakaway at the self-
same moment?

Blondy strove to move forward. But the left leg was
crazy. It let him down in a roll that carried him to the
foot of the steps. He started crawling. He had to hunch
himself forward on his hands and his right knee alone.
Like an animal galloping in slow moving pictures. There
was some sort of a chance ahead of him. For instance,
if the three of them had broken through, all the watchers
at that end of the house would be fairly sure to turn and
start in pursuit. No matter how slowly he had to drag
along, he might be able to get clear. And then if he could
find a horse—

Something crashed and went with a whang and a rattle
down the cellar steps. That was the closet door.

"Good for you, Shine!" shrilled the voice of Calico. And then a knife cut across the body of Blondy.

No, it was only the sweep of the ray from an electric pocket light. It showed him the brick wall of the cellar on one side and the jungle of a piled mass of old boxes on the other. Through a gap among the boxes Blondy wriggled.

He lay down in the dark, there. He lay down on his left side. The pain of the pressure on his wounded leg could not match his exhaustion or the exquisite relief of lying still for the moment. It was as though not only blood but nerve-strength along with it had rushed out of the wound and left him a shuddering wreck.

He remembered how Tenner had acted after the bullet struck him. Perhaps he would be the same way, unmanned, weak as a child.

Other footfalls were streaming down the cellar steps. Lamplight wavered suddenly through the room. And then a voice came bawling from the other side, from that point at which the three had made their exit: "Mr. Baldwin! Mr. Baldwin! Bill Roan, McGuire and Layden all come running out of the old cellar door a minute ago. I think I put lead into Layden. But they all run through us. They come dodging different ways. The light wasn't no good. You want all of us to go chasing them?"

Baldwin's voice thundered: "Let them go and be damned. We want The Streak! And he's somewhere here in this cellar. Streak, do you hear me? Do you give up the game, you dog? Will you come crawling to me now, you murderer?"

There were men all through the cellar. Blondy could hear them moving and breathing. He began to forget his exhaustion and grow aware of the pain in his leg.

After all, there was nothing for it except surrender. There was nothing except to sing out that he surrendered, and then to crawl out into the light.

So it would seem, in the end, that he had done what Baldwin commanded and gone crawling to his feet, like a dog to the whip hand of the master.

Afterwards, they would tell Mary Layden about it. She would not change face, but she would remember how she had seen him in the kitchen, blank-faced, sick with fear when the name of Calico Charlie had come to his lips.

Under her quietness there was all of this strength of which he never had dreamed in the first days.

Then a voice came by surprise from his own lips, saying: "I'm in here, Baldwin. Why don't some of you brave boys come and get me?"

It struck them silent for an instant. Afterwards, the sudden roar went up. Human beings had no right to make a noise like that, but only dogs in full cry, or the sea thundering against rocks.

The silence came on again. And then someone saying: "Look here! He's winged already. Look here at the blood. Here, and here. And here's where he crawled in among the boxes. There ain't any need to rush him. Leave him bleed awhile. Then we can get him cold."

"That's good sense," said the voice of Baldwin.

Afterwards, the husky whine of Shine said: "Calico Charlie wants to say something, Mr. Baldwin. He wants to say that he don't want to hunt no dead rats. He wants to find this one before it dies, and he wants to play with it a little. If all you gentlemen will go back and watch the cellar doors and just leave that little bit of lantern hangin' up there from the beam, the boss says that he'd like to go rummaging for The Streak. He wants to wipe that Streak out. He wants to leave nothin' but the yaller of it."

"Why not?" asked Perry T. Baldwin. "A very good sporting gesture I'd call it. We'll do what you ask, Calico. But when you find him back there among the boxes, shoot straight. That man is dangerous. Get back, everyone. Everybody back to the doors. If we can't see this show, at least we can hear it."

Shine's high-pitched voice answered: "You're gunna hear *screamin'*, Mr. Baldwin. You're gunna hear the yaller Streak screamin' out loud like a little gal."

They went back without protesting, only with mutterings; and then someone laughed wildly, and another man said: "The Streak dying in a pile of junk. That's a lesson for the gunmen."

Then another voice, childishly high and small and sweet came like sunshine through the cellar; Mary Layden calling: "Jim! Will you give up the fight and let me come to you?"

He sat up straight and looked wildly about him. And then that unexpected voice of his called out, gruffly: "Somebody take the girl away!"

He amazed himself. His heart was so great with the sound of her voice that he could hardly breathe. He forgot the pain that began to take his flesh apart with iron fingers. And yet he had sent her away!

Baldwin said, in the distance: "Sorry—you'll have to go, Miss Layden. This is bad work, but the law and justice must be served. Terribly sorry—some of you see her out of the house."

Then sobbing, wretched, despairing sobbing; and through the murmuring that followed a shrill cry from Jimmy: "You're cowards! You're dirty cowards! Leave me down there. I wanta die with him. I don't wanta live in a town full of dirty cowards. I don't want . . ."

Blondy heard the clap of an open hand against the face of Jimmy. And then that voice of protest was stilled, also.

He hunched himself up and waited, his back pressed against a heavy packing case. They were beginning to pull away the boxes in front of him. Shine would be doing that, like a great dog pawing away at the mouth of a hole in the ground, while Calico Charlie, like a savage little weasel, waited to run in and catch the game by the throat.

CHAPTER 32

The Moving Finger Writes

THEY had carried Tenner—or half-dragged and half-carried him out of the house. The uproar of the fighting seemed no place for a badly wounded man. They put him out on what had once been the lawn, and Doctor Morrison got to work on him. He plastered a patch over each cheek and stuffed up the bullet wounds inside. The bleeding was stopped in that manner, just as Tenner fainted.

There were only three or four standing around, by this time. Too much was happening inside and around the house. So only a handful heard the doctor say, as he tried for the pulse of Tenner: "This man is going to die. He's lost blood. And he didn't have any blood to lose. There's no more juice left in him now than there is in a dried up turnip. He's got to die, poor devil."

And then he found Tenner sitting suddenly erect under his hands, Tenner with wide, terrified, comprehending eyes.

He got suddenly to his feet. The look of the man, all blood and those staring eyes, was that of one who already had died and his ghost has come back to haunt the mortal mind. Morrison gripped him by the skinny elbows, but he kept on shaking his head and nodding it towards the house.

"He means something. He wants something, doc—dying men—" said one of the bystanders. The doctor suddenly agreed.

"We'll go on in with you," said the doctor. "If you want to get into the house. we'll go along with you. Here, help him on that side. Though why the devil he should want to get back . . ."

They helped Tenner up the steps and back into the hall of the house. In the cellar, by this time, there was a great shouting and confusion of noise; Tenner insisted on being conducted straight back down the hallway until he had reached the kitchen. There he shook away the hands of the other two and waved them off. His face was now more ghastly than ever. Some of the blood had been wiped from it, but now he was choking and rattling with every breath he drew, and the difficulty of respiration caused his eyes to thrust out. The lids were fluttering as though he were winking with some horrible, hidden meaning.

The doctor drew back into the doorway with his companion, and from the open door they saw Tenner stagger across the floor. In his blindness of pain and exhaustion he crashed straight against a chair and then floundered forward upon his knees. But recovering himself, he went on towards the stove, dropped against it half sprawling, and finally lifted an edge of the square of worn matting which was placed in front of the stove. From this he took out a yellow card, five by eight inches in size, and covered with writing.

He carried it to the kitchen table, slumped into a chair, and pulled from his pocket a lead pencil and a torn envelope. But when he strove to write on the envelope, the letters sprawled immediately off the paper.

He abandoned the attempt and began to write on the big, white-scrubbed surface of the table, while the doctor drew cautiously up behind him.

Strange sounds were rising from the cellar under the kitchen floor, but the doctor and his companion remained regardless of them, so fascinated were they by the sight of that yellow card and the words which Tenner was scrawling upon the face of the table.

Down there in the cellar, one by one Shine was dragging away the big boxes, many of them heavy packing cases which had decayed past real service, but too much thrift had retained them instead of breaking them up for firewood. Some, made heavily, were a burden even for the gigantic strength of Shine; but the Negro's exitement grew. He began to sing, panting, gasping out roaring phrases of song, laughing, yelling till a beastly slaver fell from his mouth.

And as he worked and hauled away, Calico Charlie followed, slinking, the gun in one hand and the electric torch in the other stabbing at the darkness. Vast shadows were wavering over the eyes of Blondy as the torch swayed nearer and nearer. But he was perfectly calm. He could do everything with his mind. With it he could put away the pain from his left leg. With it he could calculate just what movements he could make with the right leg and the left hand, leaving the right hand free to handle his gun. He was about to die, but he would die as the world expected The Streak to come to his end, striking out till the last.

As they came now to the very verge of the place where he lay, he rolled himself suddenly into the mouth of a long packing case which was immediately before him and crouched there. He heard Shine gasping: "They all kind of soldered to the floor, these old boxes, but away you come, box! Away you come and leave us at The Streak! Come out and fight, Streak. Where you stayin', boy? Whyn't you come out and leave us look at you? All we wanta do is pat you on the back and admire how fast you can bleed, Big Boy . . ."

His grasp shook the big packing case and dragged it back with a mighty wrench. The torch of Calico Charlie at the same time flashed red on the pool of blood where Blondy had been waiting.

That same knife of light cut now into the box and across the face of Blondy. A flying shadow cut away the light. It was the bulk of the giant Shine, diving straight at the quarry with a long knife in his hand. And Blondy lifting his gun, pressed his thumb over the hammer to let fly.

There was no missing such a target as this. He could not help but drive a bullet through that mountain of flesh. And yet his thumb would not move. In that exquisite agony of need he could not shoot at living flesh and blood!

The weight of Shine struck him, but not with the long tooth of the knife. A gun had roared at the very side of Shine as Calico Charlie, sighting his target, fired like a flash. Shine, struck by the bullet, rolled over in a convulsion of arms and legs, screaming. The sweep of one arm, like the kick of a mule, knocked the legs from under Calico Charlie and sent him sprawling, so that his gun cracked against the edge of a packing case and was knocked out of his hand and spinning away.

He was up again in a moment. His hand found the knife that Shine had dropped. The big Negro lay on his side with his knees pulled up against his belly, beating the floor with his fists in his agony. But Calico leaped over him and drove in at Blondy.

Now, surely, was the time to fire. But that strange reluctance, stronger than the fear of death, paralyzed the hand of Blondy. He struck out with the barrel of the gun. The blow was warded by the lightning hand of Calico, but it served to put the knife thrust aside. Calico Charlie landed like a fighting, snarling cat on Blondy. It was vain to try to get a grip on him. Like a cat, that was the only

way. Like a twisting, writhing, spitting cat seemed Calico
Charlie, whining with eagerness under his breath.

Blondy saw the flash of the teeth, and the glint of the
eyes. The electric torch, which had fallen on the ground,
glared upon them with a steady cone of light. With that
to guide him, Calico Charlie struck for the heart. A side-
sweep of Blondy's parrying arm knocked the blow askance.
Instead of the body it reached the wounded left thigh
and drove right in through the stiff muscles, through the
great tendons, to the bone.

There remained in the cup of Blondy's hand a long
time for thought and for action—a long tenth part of a
second as Calico tugged twice to recover the knife from the
wound it had just made. For Blondy, the long barrel of the
Colt poised, aimed at the temple of the smaller man a
stroke that would end all of Calico's battles. Then, chang-
ing his mind at the last instant, for the horror of killing
was choking him, he brought the gun down right across
the top of Calico's head.

Calico Charlie slipped limply down on his breast and
then rolled off onto the cellar floor beside Shine.

Blondy saw them with a last blurred glance. The light
whirled before his eyes. A whirlpool of black darkness
gathered in his senses. He had fainted away.

Perry T. Baldwin and the sheriff had headed the rush
towards the scene of the fighting. The brief second of
it ended as they reached the spot. Three men stretched
in the midst of blood, two of them face down, and Blondy
on his back, half in the packing case and half on the
bricks of the cellar floor.

"They're dead!" said the sheriff, somewhat moved in
spite of himself. "Three of 'em laid in a row. And the
world can thank God that the three of 'em are all gone."

"I'll just make sure of The Streak," said Perry T.
Baldwin, and put his gun to the head of Blondy.

Perry T. Baldwin was great enough to make or unmake
any dozen sheriffs in Jasper Valley, but a sudden flash of
anger made Wallace Nash kick that gun out of the famous
Baldwin hand.

"We don't shoot dead men around these parts, Baldwin!" he said, and then felt his heart shrivel as the glare
of Baldwin was turned on him. In that glare the political

death of the sheriff was decreed, and he knew it. But now the crowd washed up around them. There was no great outbreak of voices.

One man said: "They got The Streak; and he killed 'em both. If he hadn't been winged, how many more than two would he have gotten away with?"

There were plenty of hands available. They carried all those three limp weights up the stairs from the cellar and into the kitchen. Calico Charlie, with his thin skull crushed in, they laid by the side of the kitchen wall. But The Streak already had begun to stir and mutter as consciousness returned to him.

He saw things strangely and far away.

The room was thick with people, for one thing. And somehow the boy Jimmy was in there, crying through his set teeth, and Blondy felt the voice and the touch of Mary Layden. She was there too; though she could no more be there than birds could be in the depths of the sea.

Jimmy and Mary Layden—he wanted to think about them, but a voice was crying out with a terribly insistent ring, And it compelled attention to itself, and to nothing else. All other thoughts were banished by that strong shouting.

"Sheriff Nash, arrest Perry T. Baldwin. Don't let him leave the room. Arrest Perry T. Baldwin for the murder of Philip Coles!"

That was Doctor Morrison shouting.

And then a stir, and afterwards someone exclaiming: "Look here, Mr. Baldwin, you're not trying to get away, are you? You ain't afraid, are you?"

The eyes and the brain of Blondy began to clear. He pushed himself to a sitting posture with his arms suddenly filled with new strength.

People had pressed back from the center of the room, by this time. They had shrunk back towards the wall to give a field of vision in which they could see the main actors—the two dead bodies in the corner, and The Streak helpless against the wall, and Perry T. Baldwin himself, the great man of Jasper, the prophet of Greater Jasper, in the middle of the floor looking around him with stunned frightened eyes. And there was Tenner, the half-witted Tenner, seated at the table red with his own blood and writing on the white-scrubbed face of the table, scrawling words with a lead pencil. There was Doctor Morrison, finally, shouting out what he found written on a yellow card from a filing system.

"A card from the file of Philip Coles!" cried the doctor. "I tell you what's written on it. Five thousand loaned to Perry T. Baldwin; ten thousand loaned to Perry T. Baldwin. And a little over two years ago, fifty—thousand—dollars! Fifty—thousand—dollars loaned to Perry T. Baldwin! Do you hear me? Do you know what it means, you people? What do *you* say it means, Baldwin?"

Perry T. Baldwin had recovered himself. "You find a record, Doctor Morrison," he said, "of certain transactions which were cancelled long ago."

"There's only one way to cancel a debt, and that's by paying it," answered the doctor. "And every debt paid off to Philip Coles was erased from his record in his files. We all knew his system. None of these debts is cancelled, Baldwin. Instead of paying off one debt, you borrowed some more the next time. And you kept on rolling up the debt until you could make fools of the people of Jasper Valley and sell off your damned land to them at a hundred times its real value."

"I see," said Perry Baldwin, steadily, and he even smiled a little, "that the reward of public service is ingratitude and suspicion, if not actual hatred. Envy is a great sharpener of the eyes, doctor. It enables you to see things that don't exist."

"My eyes enable me to see what Tenner is writing on the face of this table," said Doctor Morrison. "Shall I read it? Will you listen? Sheriff, I want you to keep your eye on Perry T. Baldwin. I'm reading the words of Tenner, written here on this table. I'm reading the words of a dying man, I think."

Here Tenner raised his head and turned his ghastly face towards the crowd. Then he leaned again to his writing. Even that small movement had caused him to sway in his chair.

Morrison read aloud: "I, Tenner—swear and attest, being in my full sense—I saw Perry Baldwin come to the house of Coles on the night Coles was killed—I saw him go up the stairs, and I sneaked along behind. And I saw him go into the door of Coles's room and I heard him say—"

"Get out of my way!" shouted Perry T. Baldwin, shouldering suddenly towards the door. "This is a damned conspiracy—"

Sheriff Nash got to him and caught him by the shoulder.

"All right," he said. "Clear the way for him. Clear it all the way to jail for Mr. Murderer Baldwin! No wonder he wanted The Streak dead. No wonder at all! Give the law a death for a death and it closes up any case, all right. *You're* the one that made an outlaw out of The Streak, Baldwin; but you'll hang for the doing of it!"

He started on through the crowd like that, with one hand gripping the shoulder of Baldwin; and for a stunned second the people stared and loosely gave way. Then someone howled, and his voice wailed like the voice of a wolf: "Boys, we been made dogs of by the greatest skunk this side of hell. Ain't we got rope enough to give Perry T. Baldwin a necktie party?"

The answer was a yell that tore a red path through the brain of Blondy. There had been a pair of armed men guarding him till that final denunciation of Baldwin. But now they joined the rush of the crowd towards Baldwin. Force of numbers thrust him out of the hands of the sheriff. Wallace Nash was yelling: "Now, boys—damn it, you can't do this—leave go of him—he's my share——"

And Baldwin, thrust back before the crowd like foam before a wave, was torn at by hands that ripped his coat away, battered him back straight towards the place where Blondy lay.

He raised himself. Jimmy on one side and Mary Layden on the other, helped him up to save him from the feet of that rabid crew as they came trampling.

They had bandaged up that doubly wounded left leg. He could put no weight on it, but threw his left arm across the shoulders of Jimmy. That was how he stood when he shouted, and the crowd gave heed to him. They saw the horrible sprinkling of blood over his face and shirt, and his right hand dyed red as it extended above their heads.

And Blondy watched them shrink from him, making a little open space into which Perry T. Baldwin stumbled.

At last, a reaching fist had clipped him on the chin, and he faltered to one knee before The Streak.

It seemed to Blondy that a sort of light was reflected in the faces of all those people, as though he held up a torch before them. They muttered: "The Streak! He wants something! Shut up, back there! The Streak's gunna say something!"

They were hushed in a moment. They seemed to him suddenly a flock of rather helpless children.

He said: "Boys, you've been a little hard on me—in spots—this evening. Do me a favor now. Keep your teeth out of Baldwin. Let Sheriff Nash take him to jail. If you make yourselves dirty with blood, you'll never wash clean as long as you live."

They went out of that room as quietly as lambs, and Sheriff Wallace Nash took his man to jail.

Something snapped in Blondy. He went into the sleepy, warm realm of delirium and fever and roused out of it a week later with voices sounding soft and far away. Mary Layden and Buck were talking. The head of Blondy was turned towards a window and through the window, Blondy could see the two eminences, and particularly the bald top of Cannon Hill. He was in the Layden home and the sense of that hospitable place flowed gently over him. He was very sleepy, pleasantly inert and a weakness ran through him like the music of flowing water.

He heard Buck saying: "You kind of doubted, too, one time or other."

"I did," said Mary. "I don't want to think of it—But there was a moment when I thought that I saw fear in his face, Buck. And then—then everything happened that night."

"He didn't care much whether he lived or died," said Buck, "after you gave him the cold shoulder. But me—I was a fool and Bill Roan was a fool, too. Living all that time with him and never seeing the kind of fighting man that he was. And when we seen him here in Jasper, why he had ways of explaining everything that he'd done, and making it nothing.

"He laughed at what he'd done in Jasper, and Bill and me, we believed it *had* been nothing. We still kind of half thought so, till we went to the place and seen Shine and Calico Charlie, the two of them lying out side by side the way Blondy had dropped 'em. Then we knew—it kind of come over me like chills and fever. Suppose I'd made The Streak mad with something that I'd said? And I'd said plenty, only he never would get mad with a friend, d'you see?"

"He never laid the weight of a finger on a good man, Buck," said Mary Layden.

"No, I guess he never did," muttered Buck. "How soon's he gunna be all right?"

"He's very much better now," said the girl.

"And when does the marriage come?" asked Buck.

"Do you think, when the fever goes away, that he'll want me?" asked Mary Layden. "Do you think he won't remember, too clearly, that moment—it *was* only a moment, Buck—when I doubted him?"

Blondy did not hear the answer.

And then he started to lift himself in the bed. He wanted to tell them that, after all, they were utterly wrong. It was a bullet from Calico Charlie's gun that had killed Shine. It was the struggle of Shine in dying that had floored Calico. And it was chance that had given him his opportunity to crush out the life from that little spider of a man, Calico Charlie.

He started to lift himself in the bed to say this, but then he relaxed and sank back again, with a sigh.

It was no use talking. He never would be able to explain now.

Something darkened his eyes. He looked up to the face of the girl between him and the window. The soft blue of the sky closed in about her head. There would be no end to the joy of beholding her.